The Altar in the Hills
and Other Weird Tales

by
Brandon Barrows

"Suck It Up, Get It Done" first appeared in the 01 Publishing book anthology *Whispers from the Abyss*, October 2013.

"Seeker in the Dark" first appeared in the Cruentus Libri Press book anthology *Another 100 Horrors*, May 2013.

Published by Raven Warren Studios.
www.ravenwarren.com

Cover art and design by George Cotronis.
www.ravenkult.com

First edition: January, 2014.
ISBN: 9780615933597

Dedicated to HPL for opening my eyes

and to Elby for believing in me, even when I didn't
deserve it.

Table of Contents

The Altar
in the
Hills

I.

The entire sequence of events began, as is often the case, with the most innocuous of acts – in this instance, the delivery of the daily post.

Around ten-thirty in the morning on the 15th of June, 1923, Bertram Kincaid of Montville, Connecticut was at his writing desk, beginning the initial outline of a short treatise on the genealogy of one of the town's most well to do families, the Hillhouses, and commissioned by the same. The town, having been established as a separate entity from the larger New London community in large part by the efforts of James Hillhouse a century and a half earlier, remembered him fondly as the family and town's founding patriarch. His descendants and heirs had made much of that reputation and goodwill in the generations since and the current patriarch, William, intended to give back to the community by furnishing certain prominent citizens with the knowledge of exactly how important his family was. He needed assistance with a way to do so, however, since his own knowledge of any field beyond the spending of inherited money was severely limited.

Kincaid was exactly the man for this sort of work. Slightly past the quarter century mark in age, he retained the boyish looks he'd been praised for throughout childhood and a keen interest in history that he'd found no real outlet for since leaving behind the University of Connecticut with a diploma earned in less than three years. He had no desire to return to the world of education, either as instructor or student, but found his degree in history of little use for anything else. Thus, while earning a meager living contributing newspaper articles to various publications, strictly on a freelance basis, he gladly took up any sort of paying work that would allow him to put to use his research skills and delve into new areas of study, even those as mundane as the history of someone else's family.

Kincaid's study, a modest chamber on the southern side of his small, but cozy home, overlooked his garden, radiant with late spring and early summer blossoms. The open window wafted their fragrance through the room, gently rustling the stacks of research material Kincaid had organized by decades and individual Hillhouses. The knock on the front door of the house, on the opposite side of the building, broke him from the sort of happy trance he had fallen into while engrossed in his work and it was only with reluctance that he pulled himself away, rising from his desk at the second set of rapping noises.

Passing into the front hallway, Kincaid reached the door just as the knocking ceased and opened it to find his postman, Mr. Feeney, turning away to head back down the short pathway leading to the road. Upon hearing the door open, however, he paused and Kincaid asked what he could do for him.

The older man walked the few steps back to the house, a yellowed envelope in hand. "Oh, Mr. Kincaid. Thought you weren't home. This is for you," he said, handing his delivery to Kincaid, who turned it over in his hands, feeling the slightly grimy texture and trying to examine the nearly-unreadable return address.

"What happened to this letter, if I may?"

Feeney nodded, his eyes on the flagstones. "Well, that's why I knocked 'stead of just dropping it in the box, sir. The thing's been lost, up at the big sorting facility in Boston, and the postmark's nearly two years old so the postmaster asked me to offer our apologies personally and make sure it got to you this time."

Kincaid had had only scant interaction with the postman, but he knew that Feeney had been performing his duties on this route for over a decade and had always seemed a conscientious sort. His awkwardness and apparently-sincere contrition served to convince the younger man of Feeney's, and the whole of the United States Postal Service's, regret for the error.

Smiling and reaching out to shake Feeney's hand, Kincaid assured him of his understanding and thanked him for his diligence and thoughtfulness in bringing the epistle directly to him. The postman seemed much relieved and headed back off to the rest of his appointed rounds, nodding and smiling, satisfied of correcting someone else's error. Kincaid closed the door and returned to his work space.

Back in his study, the young writer cleared away a spot on his battered oaken desk to examine the letter with greater detail. The paper did, indeed, look as if it had spent a great deal of time in some forgotten, dusty corner growing brittle and yellow. Water stains had smeared and obscured the return address at some point so that nothing concrete could be discerned, though the postmark was stamped Lancaster, New Hampshire and dated August 4th, 1921. The missive was addressed to "Master Bertram Kincaid" in an elaborate, almost old-fashioned handwriting that spoke both of education and a hint of pomposity and gave Kincaid his best clue as to with whom it had originated.

Tearing open the fragile envelope, Kincaid drew out a single piece of paper, thrice-folded and covered front and back with dense lines of small, neat script, and flattened it on his desk. The temporary address scrawled at the top of the letter confirmed his suspicions. It read:

Theodore Wallace
c/o Drummer Hotel
9 Church Str.
Drummer, New Hampshire
August 3rd, 1921

Master Bertram Kincaid
44 Cottonwood Lane
Montville, Connecticut

My dear Bert —

It's been some time since I've written, though I did receive your letter this past Christmas and have simply not found the time to respond; churlish, I know, but I hope you won't hold it against me.

Life has been hectic with studies at the University and especially with work progressing apace on my master's thesis. Professor Wilmarth has taken me a bit under his wing and helped direct my researches to the proper areas of study. As you know, I'm working on a paper analyzing the integration of the old native pagan beliefs, still found in pockets around our own good old New England, with the formalized belief systems of the various Christian denominations settlers brought with them from Europe. It's really fascinating stuff, trying to determine what tidbit came from where and Wilmarth's extensive (though amateur, according to his own assessment) knowledge of New England folklore has been invaluable in focusing my work.

I've spent the last four months traveling to corners of Maine and New Hampshire, visiting villages scarcely changed from their founding, interviewing people who barely know it's the twentieth century, much less have entered it. There's a treasure trove of untapped history in these places, Bert. This is the real New England — raw and rough, with people who not only survive, but thrive away from the modern comforts we've grown so used to. And the things they tell me, why they're positively arcane. Some of the stories, tales they believe as firmly as they know the sky is blue, seem so utterly naïve you'd think this was Europe in the Dark Ages, rather than the Industrial Age of the United States. Well, I suppose you'll read all about it when my thesis is published, as I'm sure it will be.

But I'm digressing a bit from the real reason I'm writing. As you probably saw, I'm writing this from a little hamlet in the north of New Hampshire called Drummer. It's not terribly far, as the crow flies, from Lancaster, where I'll have to head to mail this tomorrow or the next day and maybe soak up a bit of civilization before moving on. If I recall correctly from our school days together, your own people hail from this general neck of the woods a few generations back.

I came here chasing a story about some sort of heathen altar built up in the hills that old Cotton Mather makes passing reference to in his Magnalia Christi Americana, though basically just to say good Christians should keep their distance. I couldn't find any other mention of it in Miskatonic's library and when I mentioned it to Wilmarth, the fact that even he knew very little about it piqued my interest a good deal. Well, the folks here are quaint, to say the least, and mostly friendly though it took more than a bit of coaxing to get any information at all about this hunk of stone.

They don't get many visitors and mentioning the thing just shut everyone down at first – fearing the thing is regarded as the healthiest attitude towards it. Once they warmed up to me, with the introduction of a sympathetic local, I at least found out its location and took a little visit up there myself, though I couldn't see what the big to do was. It's certainly man-made, but it's not covered in Satanic script or anything and the area it's in is really quite pleasant. Supposedly it's a different story under the light of a full moon; they tell me it becomes a demon-haunted place where the foulest of rituals are practiced. Nobody who'd talk to me has seen anything for themselves, of course – it's just one of those things they take as a given. I've been here over a week now and I haven't decided if I'll stay to find out the truth for myself, though the full moon is coming up in a few days or so.

Well, Bert, old boy, I should be wrapping this up. I'm sorry if I bored you with my scribblings, but I did owe you a letter and being so close to your homeland made me feel even guiltier.

I hope this letter finds you well and busy enough that my lack of writing didn't sour you on your old chum Ted. I plan to spend a couple weeks traveling down through Vermont, on Wilmarth's advice, and on my way home to Arkham, I'll take the long way around and circle down to you for a visit. If all goes to plan, I'll be seeing you sometime in mid-September and I'll be sure to bring along a jug of that hard cider I know you love.

With warmest regards,
Theodore Wallace

While reading, Kincaid couldn't help but smile. Ted Wallace was a friend from his college days who'd gone on to pursue further study at the prestigious Miskatonic University in Arkham, Massachusetts, and before long become what was known as a career student. Over the course of the last several years and a few dozen letters, interspersed with rare visits, Kincaid had watched as Wallace changed his educational focus from literature to history, to philosophy, to theology and now, apparently, to some hybrid of all those disciplines. From the tone of the letter, he was quite enjoying it, too, and Kincaid hoped his friend had found whatever information he'd been looking for.

His smile faded, however, when he remembered that this letter had been dated nearly two years ago and that the promised visit had never occurred. Kincaid had, indeed, written to Wallace around Christmas of '20 and again that following summer with no response to either note. It actually had vexed him somewhat, for a while at least, but Kincaid had gotten on with his own life and assumed his friend would write back in good time. It was slight comfort to know that Ted had responded, eventually.

Kincaid briefly considered composing a written response but, after the delay of Wallace's letter in reaching him, decided instead on a telegram. He telephoned the local Western Union office, dictating a brief message asking his friend to get in touch at his earliest convenience, directed to his Arkham address. Afterwards, Kincaid tried to return to work on his commission, but found his mind too disorganized and opted for a walk into town.

He set out for the town proper, distracted by thoughts of various scenarios that could have befallen his friend and did his utmost to dismiss the most outrageous ones. As comparatively wild as the areas Wallace had visited were, they were still contained within the wholesome and sane regions of long-settled New England, not some forgotten South American or African jungle. Kincaid forced himself to laugh at his own foolishness whenever the increasingly ridiculous visions appeared to him and the other diners at the little cafeteria on Union Street cast sideways glances at him each time.

Returning to his home around three in the afternoon, Kincaid was surprised, but pleased, to find a telegram envelope pinned to his doorway. He'd expected no response for at least a day or two; apparently his note had not only found Wallace, but perhaps jolted him into realization of his own rudeness at ignoring a supposedly good friend. Despite himself, Kincaid grinned as he tore open the small, yellow envelope, anticipating yet another apology for the lack of communication. It died as quickly as his eyes absorbed the scanty message.

REGRET TO INFORM - WALLACE ABSENT SINCE SPRING '21. NO FORWARDING ADDRESS. WHO CAN COLLECT HIS BELONGINGS?
PATRICIA MORRILL

Mrs. Morrill was Wallace's landlady, whom Kincaid had met on a couple different occasions while visiting

Arkham. The fact that she'd not seen or heard from Wallace since around the time, according to his letter, he'd begun his travels was worrying and the fact that she seemed only concerned with being rid of his things left behind was angering, if only briefly. Kincaid decided he couldn't blame her on that front, however; Wallace was her renter, not her child, and he supposed she had tenants come and go on a regular basis. Best not to become too attached and so forth.

Realizing he'd been standing on the doorstep for some time, Kincaid let himself inside and quietly closed the door behind him, gears churning in his mind. Before this morning, he hadn't thought about Ted Wallace in months; now, worry over his fate threatened to consume him. It was an odd thing how old allegiances, regardless of how long dormant, could come to the forefront again as strong as ever. He and Ted had once been the best of friends all through school and even after; until Wallace's disappearance, they remained close despite the distance and relative infrequency of contact.

Kincaid caught himself at the thought of Wallace as having "disappeared." The idea had crept into his mind without his notice and he didn't care for it, much as the evidence available to him pointed in that direction. He shook his head slightly, as if to cast the offending concept away, and he headed towards his study. He stopped at the door, however, and instead turned back the way he'd come, entering the front room where he dialed a long distance telephone call before he could dwell on the cost or the absurdness of his worry.

The operator connected him to Miskatonic University, where he asked the switchboard girl to kindly connect him with Professor Albert Wilmarth of the English department. She informed him that Wilmarth did not have his own telephone line, but took a message and assured Kincaid that she would have the professor call him when he had time. Thanking her, Kincaid disconnected and returned, once again, to his study where he spent a fruitless hour attempting to work on the Hillhouse family history.

The passing of another ninety minutes found Kincaid gazing out of the window near his desk, admiring how the setting sun cast a splendid array of golden light and crisp shadows through the spread of his garden, when the ringing of the telephone broke his half-dreaming reverie. He leapt from his seat and made his way to the front room with considerable haste, lifting the 'phone's receiver before the second ring had quite finished.

"This is Kincaid," he answered and exchanged some minor pleasantries with Professor Wilmarth, thanking him sincerely for taking the time to return his call before explaining his concern for Wallace after receiving the delayed letter.

Wilmarth confided that he, too, held concerns for Wallace but unfortunately had not heard anything from his erstwhile protégé in some time, either.

"We discussed his travel plans in great detail," he continued. "Ted seemed quite pleased I was able to suggest specific places for him to conduct his research and together we made a list of villages and towns in out of the way places that I considered best-suited to the kind of things he wanted to hear about.

"He set off in mid-April and made a stop in Kingsport, a bit north of here, before taking a train up to Portland where he hired a car so as to more freely explore the interior. Maine's got quite a few little hamlets scattered about that only rarely have outside contact, and I know he found a few gems up there; he sent me notes whenever he passed through a town with a real post office, and they were all very excited. From what he told me, it seemed like he was having the time of his life.

"Once he passed into New Hampshire, the letters got a bit farther apart – he'd been sending about one a week or so, which I gathered was the average length he spent in each place. Not really surprising, though; the north hills of New Hampshire aren't too well-populated and I doubt there were many real post offices to be found. He'd only use those, you know. He didn't trust a general store to pass along the mail of some stranger passing through. Even in this day and age, suspicion of outsiders runs deep in those kinds of places. There's a real sense of tribalism in those isolated little communities that men like you and I just can't truly grasp.

"Anyway, the last I heard from Ted, he was spending time in a place called Drummer and he said that he'd found not only some wonderful tales, but an actual physical remnant of some old culture. We'd talked about this supposed altar up there before he left, but I never guessed he'd really find it. Some time, when I've got a chance to get away, I'd like to see it for myself."

Throughout this, Kincaid had been listening intently, but not hearing anything he deemed of importance. When Wilmarth mentioned Drummer, however, his instincts went wild and that part of the brain responsible for intuition matched up perfectly with the logical mind.

"Drummer, you say…" he began and explained to the academic how the letter he, too, had received from Wallace had been written during his stay in that village. He gave Wilmarth every detail Wallace had provided and, when the professor had a moment to digest it, finished by telling him how Wallace had promised to visit but never arrived.

"Yes, that is strange," Wilmarth agreed. "He spoke very highly of you. Thought you and I would get along quite nicely, actually. Well, unfortunately, though," he paused and cleared his throat, resuming in a tone drenched in awkwardness. "Unfortunately, I'll have to end this. It's getting rather late and we've talked long enough that I'll end up having to explain this bill to the department head. Please do let me know if you hear from Ted, though. I'll be as eager for news as I imagine you are."

Kincaid thanked the professor once again for his time and promised to contact him as soon as he knew anything, then hung up the telephone and sat down to brood in the growing darkness.

The pieces he'd gathered fit together in a way Kincaid did not care for at all. Wallace not contacting him for extended periods was not wholly out of character; he had always been a bit self-absorbed and tended to throw himself fully into projects, as evidenced by his planned tour of New England's remote corners. Staying out of touch with Wilmarth, however, was more worrisome – as Wallace's mentor in the field of folklore, it would not benefit him any to keep quiet on that front. And perhaps strangest of all was Wallace's abandoning of his possessions left behind in Mrs. Morrill's house. In another man, this might not have been unusual, but Wallace was quite materialistic, especially in regards to the dozens of rare books and manuscripts he'd collected over the years and spent huge quantities of his family estate on. He had even, during their college days, managed to obtain a battered and rat-eaten copy of the *Necronomicon*, and the two of them had spent more than a few nights shivering with delightful fear as they translated the faded Latin script. There was no way Wallace would permanently leave his treasures by choice.

Kincaid sat in the dark, pondering, until well past midnight. Wallace had no family his friend was aware of; that no one had investigated his disappearance, as Kincaid was now convinced it was, for nearly two years proved that if Wallace had kin, they were not close, anyway. He didn't know who his friend's compatriots at the university might be beyond Wilmarth, and it was obvious from their discourse that the professor, while concerned, had a life and probably family of his own to worry about. That left Kincaid and Mrs. Morrill, the landlady, to worry about Wallace; he laughed sardonically at the woman's telegram.

No, there was only Kincaid himself.

II

A train of an older style carried Kincaid from Manchester, New Hampshire's largest city, north to Lancaster. He was actually rather surprised to learn that the town had a train station, but it was explained by a fellow passenger that Lancaster's main industry was lumber and that it was a necessity. Kincaid was more than glad to hear it, having imagined bumping along rustic back roads in some hired coach.

Before leaving Montville he'd contacted his client, William Hillhouse, and begged a deadline extension, citing the need to clear up a personal problem and offering a discount on the service that he could ill-afford. Hillhouse blustered and made a show of being disappointed with Kincaid's "lack of commitment and professionalism," but it was obvious that he was secretly pleased with the idea of paying less than previously agreed for his vanity project. In the end, he magnanimously granted Kincaid's request and wished him well on his journey.

Two days by rail from Montville to Manchester were followed by another day ending in Lancaster, putting Kincaid within proverbial throwing distance of Drummer, thirty some-odd miles further east into the hills. He spent the night in an elderly, but comfortable, hotel on the main drag where he learned both that a bus route traveled between Lancaster and Drummer and, from the guest register, that Wallace had stayed here for a single night the day after his letter had been written.

Morning saw Kincaid waiting for the bus bright and early, his single traveling bag in hand, though disappointed when he learned from the driver that

Drummer was the second stop on the line and that he must sit through a trip somewhat north, to the town of Littleton, before the route swung back towards the southeast and his goal. Three hours of jouncing ride along bumpy roads, past dense and mostly-untouched New England greenery, brought him to the little village; a parting warning from the driver left him with the knowledge that the bus only ran this way three times a week. It being Wednesday, if Kincaid missed the Friday pick up, he would be stuck until Monday or have to find his own way back to civilization. Kincaid nodded his understanding and bid the driver safe travels.

The day was warm and sunny and the time shortly after noon; Kincaid stretched his cramped legs, back and arms and took in the sights around him. The village was quaint and seemed to have a slightly dreamy quality – as if it was not so much a real place as what he'd imagined such a place would look like. A few villagers passed by him on the hard-packed dirt street and seemed mildly curious, if not actively inquisitive. A young couple, in response to his inquiry, directed him a street over to the Drummer Hotel, the only public lodgings in the area.

He found the place situated between an apparently-permanently closed up cobbler shop on one side and a private residence on the other and across from the church that gave the street its name. The church seemed to be the best-kept building in the village, as is often the case in such places. By contrast, the Drummer Hotel was an ancient affair with a sagging gambrel roof and peaked gables and appeared it could have pre-dated the settling of the area, it was so old.

Had there been any other option, he would not have trusted to stay under that decrepit roof.

Kincaid entered the shabby lobby, placing his bag on the floor by the desk, and looked around for anyone who appeared employed there. No bell was in sight, but cautious calls of "hello" eventually brought an elderly man in a faded uniform out of the back room, who deigned to ask under what name he'd like to register.

"Bertram Kincaid," he answered, utterly unprepared for the response.

"Kincaid?!" the old man spat, his formerly bored countenance transforming into one of disgust. "Finally come back heah, have ye?"

Kincaid was confused and said so, pleading ignorance at the man's meaning and explaining that he had never before set foot in New Hampshire, much less the village of Drummer. The old man fished a grimy pair of spectacles from somewhere beneath the counter and squinted at Kincaid.

"My mistake, then. My mistake." He pushed the register towards the younger man. "Take my advice, though – don't go 'round this town proclaiming ye'self a Kincaid if ye plan to stay longuh than it'd take fuh folks to run ye out."

Kincaid signed his name and asked, "Why is that?"

"Nevah you mind!" the clerk snapped as he grabbed the heavy book from Kincaid's grasp.

Kincaid made to protest, asking if he might peruse the book for the name of a friend who'd visited some time ago, but was refused. The old man tossed a key onto the desk and disappeared into the back area without another word, leaving Kincaid to find his room on his own. He had heard many things about these rustic New Englanders, chiefly that they were simple and superstitious, but friendly. It seemed only the former statements were true.

He lifted his solitary bag and turned towards the corner of the lobby where a narrow flight of stairs creaked its distress at his every step upwards. The key he'd been unceremoniously presented with was engraved with the number four and the room it matched was not hard to find. It seemed there were only four total and Kincaid's was the last on the right, down a dismal, dusty corridor which showed no signs of having recently hosted any life of a higher order than dust mites.

The room was a rear one, with a single, grimy window facing out of the back of the building towards a copse of dense conifers that, despite the noonday sun, managed to cast the area behind the hotel in deep shadow. The space was furnished with cheap, filthy pieces that were probably old before Kincaid's birth. He sighed. Humble as his own home was, it seemed a palace compared to this sad affair; he consoled himself with the idea that he would be gone from this place within a few days.

Forgoing unpacking his scant luggage, Kincaid secured the door to the room once more and headed back down to the lobby to find some sort of luncheon before beginning his investigation into the possible location of his friend and the strange doings Wallace had alluded to. Once on the first floor, however, there was no sign the hotel clerk had returned from whatever hole he was hiding in and Kincaid's polite calls, then mild shouts, went unanswered. Unable to do anything more than shrug impotently, he pushed open the wobbly double doors of the hotel and stepped out of that dreary place back into the wholesome sunshine.

In the packed-dirt street, only a very few people could be seen going about their business, mostly of an older age who were likely retired. Kincaid wondered what occupations were available for younger people in this area, so far from any convenient place of employment. He didn't imagine very many traveled to Lancaster on a daily basis, and he had seen no businesses in town beyond the hotel and the closed cobblers.

A passerby easily three times Kincaid's age, stooped but cheerful, provided directions to the general store where, he said, the younger man would find the only lunch counter in town. Glad to have found an amicable soul after his experience with the hotel clerk, Kincaid thanked the man, shook his hand and introduced himself. At this, the septuagenarian recoiled as though struck and his countenance closed off as if Kincaid's introduction had been the foulest of insults. The man turned on his heel and tottered off as quickly as he was able, ignoring Kincaid's shock and entreaties to return. Whatever negativity was attached to the name "Kincaid" in these northern hills seemed not to be confined to the hotel clerk. Kincaid resolved, if at all possible, to be tighter lipped about his full identity.

Finding the general store easily with the directions given, Kincaid was greeted at the door by a heavyset, middle-aged fellow sweeping the wooden porch. The shopkeeper, after welcoming him to the town warmly, sent him to the back of the store where a morose girl of about sixteen, bearing a strong resemblance to the proprietor, took his order and swiftly prepared for him a simple sandwich of salt meat and an excellent local cheese. While he ate, Kincaid attempted to engage the girl in conversation about the area, but earned nothing more than the occasional grunt in response and soon gave up.

Finishing his meal, Kincaid took the bill slip the girl had slapped down on the counter to the cash register by the door, where the owner had taken up station. Kincaid paid for his meal, as well as purchasing a box of crackers and more native cheese to sustain him in the evening, as he had doubts of obtaining dinner at his hotel. Through their transaction, the storekeeper said barely a word beyond the minimum needed to conduct the business and Kincaid wondered at this change of attitude from the friendliness the man had exhibited barely twenty minutes earlier. As Kincaid exited the building, he noticed the Drummerian who'd directed him here leaning against the side of the building and knew. The old man narrowed an eye and spit a phlegmy wad into the dirt a few paces in front of the hapless young man, then turned and disappeared into the alleyway.

Word traveled fast, apparently, and if he was honest, Kincaid was not surprised. There couldn't be more than a couple of hundred residents of Drummer, and in a place as insular as this, what one decided was true was generally upheld by his kith and kin, especially when the target was a stranger with a name of dubious local reputation. Still, both the old fellow and the storekeeper were of an older generation; surely there must be people about not so set in their ways and perhaps more open-minded. He shook his head to clear away the unpleasant experience and made his way up the street towards a cluster of buildings he'd yet to explore.

Kincaid spent the rest of the afternoon, and the early part of the evening, fruitlessly. Undertaking a systematic exploration of the village, going down one side of each of the town's four streets then back up the other, he discovered that Drummer was not nearly as empty as it had first appeared. Regardless of where he encountered natives, however – the feed store, a small volunteer firehouse, a building that passed as a town clerk's office, even a few private residences that he dared to knock on the doors of – or to what degree of friendliness people at first exhibited, at the explanation of his reasons for visiting Drummer they became immediately taciturn. The mere mention of the mysterious altar, or even the visit of his friend Wallace, brought out the rustics' distrust so powerfully, it could not be overcome by any amount of reasoning, cajoling or pleading. And though he was careful not to give his surname to anyone, Kincaid suspected those Drummerians who would not speak to him at all, or became abusive when he approached them, had been informed of exactly who he was, or at least was thought to be. Perhaps word did not spread quite so quickly as Kincaid had feared, but all the same he knew that it would not be long before all avenues in Drummer were closed to him. That knowledge was mightily disheartening.

Trudging back towards his hotel just after dusk, his way lit by the nearly-full moon which shone high above and an electric torch he carried, Kincaid was surprised by a hushed voice that called to him by name from the porch of a darkened house a short distance away. Turning on his heel, he shined the torch towards where the voice had come from, revealing a well-dressed, bespectacled and bookish-looking man in his late middle age who threw up his hands at the sudden glare and cried out in surprise. Kincaid pointed the light down a bit, but warily kept his distance and asked by whom he was being addressed.

The other man squinted, his eyes still dazzled, and opened the door to the house, waving a hand to indicate Kincaid should follow him. Kincaid was naturally hesitant, his experiences in Drummer so far disinclining him towards trusting anyone here. After a moment's pause, the older man came down off of the porch and offered his hand in greeting to Kincaid. "My name is Sherman Woolley, Mr. Kincaid, and I understand your reluctance but, please – someone will see us." Kincaid considered for another half moment, then nodded and followed Woolley inside.

Woolley secured the door behind them then moved further into the house, leaving Kincaid to follow once again. The interior of the little house was in a late colonial style, and tastefully decorated with framed maps of the New England states and small paintings done in an amateur, but not untalented hand. It seemed very much like a home Kincaid could imagine himself living in and he felt at once at ease, despite having just met his host. The picture he was already forming of Woolley was of a man of breeding and intellect, and he hoped fervently that he was not wrong.

Kincaid followed Woolley to the end of the front hall and a small sitting room, where Woolley lit an oil lamp and offered his guest a seat in a worn, but comfortable-looking chair. Kincaid sat, but Woolley remained standing, looking as if he'd forgotten something. Evidently putting it aside he asked, "Can I offer you something to drink, Mr. Kincaid? A bite to eat, perhaps?" Kincaid shook his head and politely refused, but Woolley pressed. "Are you certain? Your dining options are severely limited. I'm just an old bachelor, but I do alright around the kitchen, if I say so myself."

Kincaid found himself warming up to his host quickly and assented gratefully. Woolley excused himself to another part of the house and returned a few minutes later with a pot of tea and a plate of sandwiches. As he poured for the both of them, Woolley said, "I apologize very much for the cloak and dagger way I've invited you in, Mr. Kincaid, but I fear it was necessary."

Kincaid tried his tea, enjoying the faint taste of jasmine. "I hate to ask why, as I think I can guess."

Woolley nodded and sipped his own drink. "I'm sure you can. I am an outsider, too, though I've lived here for a number of years. Still, people find some of my 'fancy ways' suspect; being seen to openly associate with someone they've deemed undesirable would make my life unnecessarily difficult, so you have my apologies again for the clandestineness.

"For all that, folks around here are not bad people, let me assure you. Not at all; they are the veritable salt of the earth. But they are, I'm afraid, very much set in their ways and as superstitious as an old New England community can be. Were you not who you are, and here for the reasons you are, you would find Drummer a very different place to visit, though perhaps not as interesting." He smiled.

Swallowing a bite of sandwich, Kincaid set down his plate. "I'm sure that's true, sir, but you didn't go to this trouble just to tell me that."

Woolley's smile was replaced by a look Kincaid didn't know how to interpret. "No," he admitted, standing up to peek out of the curtain of the room's only window. Securing the hanging once again, he returned to his seat. "This is a very small town, Mr. Kincaid. Just a village, really. Nothing is secret for long, I'm afraid, and your inquiries are upsetting people. I understand why you're here – I had a similar conversation with your friend Mr. Wallace some time ago."

Kincaid's heart leapt in his chest at this, the first real clue to his friend's whereabouts, but Woolley held up a hand to forestall any interruption and resumed. "We really don't get many visitors here, and few stay more than a couple of hours to conduct whatever business brought them, so I make every effort to meet and converse with those who do. People know this and I was told very early on about your visit and the questions you were asking people. The same goes for your friend. I found Mr. Wallace's project quite interesting and helped him as much as I could – I thought it would be a wonderful distraction in my retirement."

Sensing something was expected of him, Kincaid said, "Retirement? You don't seem quite-"

"Old enough?" Woolley nodded in agreement. "Well, as I said, I'm not originally from Drummer. I was born near Burlington, Vermont and schooled in Boston. I spent the first half of my professional life teaching grammar school in various places around Massachusetts before being offered the job as schoolmaster here. It seemed like an adventure, at the time – a chance to open up the mental vistas of children with little opportunity for education. The first few years were just that, and very rewarding. But then the county decided there weren't enough students to justify their paying for a school in every town and village, so my little school house was closed. Now students from four or five different communities are bussed to the district school in Lancaster."

Kincaid nodded politely, though he was eager to get back to the topic of his missing friend. Woolley took the hint and apologized. "I'm sorry; this isn't germane to the present situation, is it? I do ramble sometimes." Kincaid assured him it was quite all right, but invited Woolley to tell him more about Wallace and the altar.

"Right. Yes, Wallace and the altar. Well, the altar," he paused again, gathering his thoughts as his brows furrowed. "The altar – I'm not entirely sure what to tell you about it. It's just a lump of stone up in the hills about six miles south of town, as far as I know. The townspeople have a lot of folklore about it – vague, evasive on details, of course, but singularly agreed upon that it is somehow evil. The thing was most definitely made by human hands – no natural phenomenon I'm aware of has ever created any sort of writing, illegible as it is, even by accident – but it hardly seems the thing that Indians of these parts would have built. The very few I've talked to tell stories similar to those the white folks have been telling for generations. That's doubtless where they picked it up, but it's somehow become more real to them than it perhaps should be. Everyone *knows* that unwholesome things happen up there around that altar on the full moon – but, of course, nobody has ever *seen* it, though they'll swear a great uncle or a neighbor's cousin or what have you has.

"Now, I told all of this to your friend Ted Wallace, too, though in greater detail than I think you care about. He was very excited; said it was wonderful material for his paper he was writing. I did warn him, though, as I'll warn you – if you choose to visit the altar, don't let the villagers know. And for God's sake, don't take anything away from the site itself. Mr. Wallace took some charcoal rubbings of the thing, hoping to suss out whatever symbols people claimed to see, and LeMeiux, the hotelier whom you've doubtless met, damned near had a fit. He wouldn't even allow Wallace back into his place with them and Wallace asked me to store them here for him until he was ready to leave town."

Kincaid leaned forward in his seat, his interest further piqued and temporarily forgetting his friend's plight. "Do you still have them? I'd be curious to see, if so."

Woolley shook his head. "No. Wallace came and got them the day before he planned to leave."

"Planned?" That sounded ominous to Kincaid; a gnawing feeling grew in his belly, despite the meal he'd had. "What do you mean 'planned'? He's no longer in Drummer, is he? People wouldn't keep him here against his will, even if he did disturb their little altar, or keep it from a worried friend come looking for him, if he chose to stay, would they?"

Shifting uncomfortably, Woolley didn't immediately answer. He let out a great sigh and met Kincaid's eye with his own. "Mr. Kincaid, that's … complicated to answer."

Worry and sudden anger got the best of Kincaid, who leapt to his feet and shouted, "Damn your complications! Where is Ted Wallace?!"

With a soothing manner practiced from years of teaching, Woolley calmed Kincaid and when both were once again seated, and the younger man civil, said, "I believe I can arrange to show you, but you will have to trust me."

Kincaid's anger began to rise again. "Trust you? How can I when you've known this whole time!? Is the entire town in on this cruel joke?"

Woolley sighed again. "I know it's difficult, but please, try. You've had a very long day, and there's nothing we can do tonight, anyway." Woolley rose and Kincaid did the same. "Go back to the hotel, Mr. Kincaid, and try to get some rest. I will come see you tomorrow afternoon and if I am successful, at least some of your questions will be answered."

Kincaid protested, but Woolley was firm; nothing would happen tonight. Angry, frustrated and disappointed, but realizing there was no point in further antagonizing the one ally he'd found, Kincaid accepted Woolley's assurances and returned to the hotel, where he flopped down onto the ancient, sagging mattress and immediately dropped off into a deep, dreamless sleep.

III.

Kincaid woke early the next morning, his body aching from the insufficient bedding, and refreshed himself as much as he was able by splashing his face, head and shoulders with the sulfurous-smelling water from the ancient porcelain sink in the dismal bathroom down the hall from his room. After dressing and breakfasting on his supply of cheese and crackers, he went downstairs to discover with surprise the sour-faced landlord sitting behind the desk reading a newspaper. Inquiring of the man where coffee and a newspaper of his own might be obtained, Kincaid was rewarded with a grunted suggestion that he try wherever he had come from before invading the hotelman's peace and quiet. With a small sigh of frustration, Kincaid thanked the man anyway and decided to try the general store where he'd found lunch the day before.

His reception was no warmer at the Drummer Grocery and Dry Goods, though he was at least able to obtain a cup of coffee. Newspapers were to be found, as well, but after learning they were all several days old, he declined, paid for the beverage, purchased a sandwich for his mid-day meal and departed.

Woolley had said the evening before that he would visit at the hotel sometime in the afternoon. Presented with the choice of remaining in that dreadful pile or exploring the area, Kincaid had little trouble in deciding. Since there was nothing to see in the town that he had not already, he struck out in the general direction that Woolley had indicated he could find the mysterious altar that was at the heart of all this trouble.

Following a weather-worn and ill-maintained road south, Kincaid hiked into the gently rolling hills through pine, fir and birch trees, progressing slightly, but steadily, higher as the road grew fainter and fainter before disappearing altogether. The day was warm and pleasant, though the sun was partially hidden by a light cloud covering for which Kincaid was grateful; he was not dressed for this kind of activity. He regretted not bringing along a water supply, though he relished the fresh air, the crunching of leaves and needles under his shoes and the singing of the birds in the trees all around him. He hadn't realized how sick of spirit he'd become, even after less than twenty-four hours in Drummer, and felt a measure of refreshment enter his mind, body and soul.

A couple of hours' tramping southwards brought him to a steeper incline than he would have guessed was to be found after traversing the gentle hills all morning. The trees had thinned somewhat and a narrow trail between sizeable rock fragments led further up. Kincaid turned back the way he'd come and gazed out over the little valley he hadn't realized Drummer sat in, the town itself just barely visible through the trees. Fifteen minutes' rest and half of his sandwich later, Kincaid began the more arduous climb before him.

The rocky path proved somewhat easier to mount than was expected and Kincaid made good time, reaching the summit in less than thirty minutes. At the top, he was presented with a sort of wooded plateau into which the trail he'd been following continued. Only a short distance into the woods, however, the foliage opened up to reveal a small glade, the center of which was dominated by the altar Kincaid had come to see.

The thing was of hexagonal shape, the corners worn smooth by the passage of time and the badgering of the elements. It was a bit more than four feet in height, about as long, but only half that distance wide. Unbidden, the thought that it was near perfect a platform for a human body sprung to mind and Kincaid shivered, despite the warmth of the day and his own exertions. The top surface of the altar was rough and pitted from the beating wind and weather had given it and, walking around to examine it from all angles, Kincaid noticed that though the sides were in better shape than they had a right to be, they, too, were in less than pristine condition. While not especially knowledgeable in such areas, Kincaid decided that the altar must be several thousands of years old if it was a day, but despite that, the hunk of stone seemed more a curiosity than an object of terror and he clucked his tongue at the foolishness of old New England superstition.

Sitting cross-legged on the ground several feet away from the altar, Kincaid rested his elbows on his knees and studied it further, all the while going over the past few days' events and the pieces of information he'd obtained. While he sat, the clouds overhead came together enough to obscure the sun, plunging the little clearing into shadow. When they parted again a moment later, a beam of light landed squarely on the altar; simultaneously Kincaid was struck by something Woolley had said the night before. The retired teacher had made mention of illegible writing on the stone, but Kincaid – despite a fairly close scrutiny – had seen nothing even remotely of the sort.

Leaping to his feet, Kincaid approached the altar slowly, half-squatting as he circled it, and made an even closer study than he had already. As before, however, he saw no evidence of any sort of writing, symbols, hieroglyphics or anything that did not appear to be either an ancient tool mark from the thing's original construction or damage from natural processes. He stood back up and, rubbing his chin in thought, decided to question Woolley further on this point. The man held at least some answers, of that Kincaid was sure, and this was only one item that needed further clarification. He had also had no chance to ask about the mystery of the Drummerians' aversion to his surname, and he made mental note to bring this up, as well.

Kincaid returned to his seat at the edge of the clearing and closed his eyes in thought. Wallace had said in his letter that the altar lay in a pleasant area, and Kincaid could not deny there was a great deal of charm to these wooded hills, but he could not agree entirely. There was something more than a bit ominous about this piece of carved stone that did not belong in this place or time. Opening his eyes again, he checked his pocket watch, which showed half-past eleven; Kincaid decided he had better start back towards Drummer, for fear of missing Woolley's visit, though he was reluctant to depart this place so soon. He hated leaving mysteries unsolved, but had to admit to himself that this was not one he could unravel on his own.

Returning to town, Kincaid found the way down to be easier and faster going than the way up and made good time, reaching the Drummer Hotel at half past one. He washed the stains of his excursion away with more of the hotel's foul-smelling water and changed into his spare clothing, just finishing as a knock sounded on the door to his room.

He was not surprised to find Woolley in the hallway, though the man's nervousness was unexpected. After exchanging greetings, Woolley invited Kincaid to follow him outside, explaining that while he had made the arrangements as promised, they must hurry before "she" changed her mind. Kincaid, perplexed, asked whom he meant but Woolley had gone silent. The younger man was irritated, but chose not to push his benefactor; Woolley was the only one who had aided him, and he could not risk upsetting or insulting the man.

They traveled by foot for a distance of a little more than a mile, following the road heading east out of town until coming to a small house, set back a short ways from the road and surrounded by well-tended vegetable gardens and a low, white-washed fence. The whole effect was of a house that did not quite belong to its environment, but it was a pleasant setting, nonetheless.

Pausing at the end of the walkway leading to the building, Woolley placed a hand on Kincaid's arm and spoke at last. "Watch yourself in here, Mr. Kincaid. I say this to you as a friend – she is fiercely protective and will not hesitate to make trouble for you, if she perceives you as doing so for her or those she claims as her own. Whatever she asks, just agree, whatever she says, just take as Gospel and thank your lucky stars she agreed to this meeting. It was no small task obtaining her assent, I assure you."

Baffled, Kincaid had no chance to ask the questions on his mind as Woolley stepped smartly to the door and wrapped lightly with his knuckles. A moment passed before the portal creaked open to reveal a small, neatly dressed, and extremely elderly woman who nevertheless emanated a sense of power, confidence and control. This was her domain – let one forget that at his own peril!

Woolley smiled broadly and nodded politely while gesturing towards Kincaid. "Mrs. Powell, this is the young man we spoke of earlier."

Kincaid stepped forward and extended a hand in greeting, but was met only with a hard, appraising stare from the woman. She looked long and fiercely at him, but just when he feared she would find him somehow wanting, she stepped back and threw the door to her home open wide, muttering, "Alright, in with you, then, if you're coming."

Woolley thanked the woman profusely and gestured for Kincaid to precede him. The young man did so, and entered the abode under the watchful gaze of its mistress, careful to wipe his feet on the mat by the door. This earned him an approving nod from Mrs. Powell, but left him under no pretenses of having won her over.

The house was as small as it appeared from the outside, sparsely decorated and seeming to consist of two rooms on the ground floor – a sitting room and a kitchen – with a narrow staircase at the end of the hall leading upwards. Towards this Mrs. Powell hobbled, leading the men to the bottom and jerking a thumb upwards. "The room on the left, Woolley. The opposite's mine and if I so much as suspect that door's been touched, you'll regret it 'til your dying day." The man thanked her again for her time and generosity then led the way upstairs, Kincaid bringing up the rear.

The second floor of the house was barely half the size of the first, and the sharply sloping ceiling gave it a cramped feeling that made Kincaid somewhat claustrophobic. Woolley stood by the door to the left of the stairs, a hand on the knob, and the other held up to give Kincaid pause. The look on the man's face seemed genuinely sorrowful to Kincaid and for an instant, he did not want to know what was on the other side of that portal.

"Mr. Kincaid, I warn you – what you're going to see will not be easy. Steel yourself." So saying, Woolley opened the softly creaking door and stepped aside for Kincaid.

The room was as small as Kincaid had expected, and dominated by an old-fashioned post bed which took up more than half of it. Sunlight peeked through a single small window opposite the door, insufficient to light the room beyond the bare necessity to navigate the space. Seated in a rocking chair, staring out of the window, was a crumpled figure that made no indication it was aware of the intrusion.

Unsure of how to proceed, Kincaid greeted the figure and moved slowly closer, extending a hand in greeting and introducing himself. The person in the chair continued to face away from him and Kincaid could glean few details beyond the pale, sickly complexion and the rampant growth of beard that the half-hidden face sported. A creaking floorboard startled him until he realized it was only Woolley entering the room.

The former-teacher gently brushed past Kincaid, saying, "I think we'll have to help him turn." He squeezed behind the rocking chair and, warning the occupant he was doing so, gently altered its direction until both were facing Kincaid. The young man's jaw dropped as his heart did the same.

"Ted!" he cried out and sank to his knees before his friend, who still made no acknowledgement he was aware of his guests. Kincaid took Wallace's hands in his own, disturbed by the brittleness of the skin and the bird-like lightness of the digits, and looked the damaged man in the eye, searching for any hint of recognition. He found none.

Turning to Woolley, Kincaid's face wore a look of anguish that the older man felt nearly as keenly as the guilt he felt for not adequately warning his new friend. "What's – what has happened to him?" Kincaid asked, choking on the words.

Woolley shook his head sadly, avoiding Kincaid's gaze. "His neck was broken. Your guess is as good as mine as to how. He was found near the hill where the altar lies, the morning he had planned to move on from Drummer. It was early in the day and the men who discovered him surmised that he had tripped in the darkness and fallen, perhaps while running – which would account for the force he evidently fell with."

Kincaid was beside himself, a mixture of sorrow and rage churning in his belly. "Even if that was so, if this was merely an accident, why is he still here? Why did no one track down anyone who knew him and could take him home?"

Woolley sat down on the bed next to Wallace, a hand on the insensate man's shoulder. "I tried, as did the county sheriff. At least I was told he did. But Wallace had not spoken of any family and he had nothing in his possession which could lead to any kin. I wrote to Miskatonic University without any reply. Sheriff Coggins wanted to ship the poor man off to the state hospital for the deranged but, by then, Mrs. Powell had heard of his plight and 'adopted' him. Her own son, James, was killed in a logging accident many years ago and I suppose she sought to replace him."

Kincaid frowned. "You can't just 'adopt' a grown man, injured or not."

"Mrs. Powell can. She is very influential in this area. Powell money built this town, such as it is, and she is its last scion, though her means are obviously much-reduced. People defer to her and the sheriff saw no harm in letting her take care of Mr. Wallace. He obviously needed it."

Kincaid hung his head – Woolley's story made sense, after a fashion. It did not explain why Miskatonic hadn't responded to the schoolteacher's letter, though, if indeed he had sent one. He let go of his friend's skeletal hands and stood. "What did Ted have to say about this?"

Woolley shook his head. "Nothing. He has not spoken in all this time. The doctor from Lancaster said it's not related to his physical injuries. Something … something has damaged his mind. That much is obvious."

It **was** obvious. Theodore Wallace had been an intelligent, outgoing man, full of life and vigor. This shriveled husk was not that man. Perhaps it was better to let him live whatever was left of his life in the care of an old woman who needed to feel useful. There was certainly nothing that could be done for him at this stage.

For a long while, neither man said a word; only the rattling breaths of the creature in the rocking chair stirred the air. Finally, Kincaid let out a deep sigh and said, "I went to the altar this morning."

Woolley nodded. "I suspected you would. You've come a long way to find your friend; it would be odd if you didn't visit the object that brought him here."

Kincaid was not sure he wanted to progress with this line of reasoning, but Woolley was right – he had come this far, there could be no turning back.

He told Woolley of his observations of the stone, and the feelings he'd had in the area. Woolley listened as if the information was nothing new to him, but did not interrupt or seek to add anything to Kincaid's account. When done with his story, Kincaid finished by saying, "And I did not see any trace of the writing you mentioned, illegible or otherwise."

Woolley stood and turned Wallace's chair back towards the window, allowing the crippled man to see what passed for his world. When he faced Kincaid again, he was careful not to meet the other man's eyes. "No, you wouldn't have."

The evasiveness of the response triggered Kincaid's anger once more; Woolley alternated between helping him and blocking his inquiries and the younger man had had more than enough of it. He wanted straight answers and he said as much, raising his voice more than he had meant to.

The response was immediate, but it did not come from Woolley. Mrs. Powell's raspy voice called up the stairs, demanding to know what was going on and asking Woolley why they were taking so long. Woolley answered that they would be down momentarily, and turned back towards Kincaid. "We must go. We've pushed her far more than I had intended to and it would be unwise, for the both of us, to take further advantage of her hospitality."

Kincaid thought to protest but saw the truth in those words. Wallace held answers that he could not share with anyone and arguing with Woolley in an elderly woman's home would serve no purpose but to anger her and further alienate the displaced Vermonter's neighbors. After some words of goodbye to his friend, Kincaid followed Woolley down the stairs.

The two men's thanks were met by Mrs. Powell with a stare as full of menace as any living being could muster and Kincaid felt those eyes on his back long after the little house was out of sight behind them. Woolley had remained silent since leaving the Powell home and Kincaid had followed suit, formulating more questions in his mind. When the town was in sight a ways up the dusty road, Kincaid placed a hand on the other man's shoulder to stop him. "There are things you haven't told me."

Woolley did not look as if the accusation was unexpected. "No, but I swear I don't know what happened to your friend Mr. Wallace."

Kincaid looked up and down the road to ensure they were still alone, this close to Drummer proper. He spoke without looking at his companion. "I believe you, but there are other things – the writing on the altar you mentioned, why the people of this town fear me so."

Woolley looked up at the sky, which had cleared considerably after the noonday sun burned off most of the morning's clouds. "I don't think it's you they fear, exactly – rather, what they think you represent."

Kincaid asked what that could possibly be, and Woolley had to admit he didn't know. "I have lived in this town for almost twelve years, and I am still an outsider. I will always be an outsider. I have studied the records in the town clerk's office, trying to get a sense of this place's history, as well as whatever materials people will loan or give me and I still understand barely more than you do.

"Your name, 'Kincaid' – there's something about it, but I have no idea what. There was a Kincaid family here, several generations back. I've found passing references to them, mostly in inconsequential records of business transactions and the like. They arrived before Drummer was even a real town, just a collection of a few families living in proximity. There are birth and death records in the town's books for every family of that period I can find – but none for the Kincaids. And after the War Between the States, there's nothing at all. It's as if they were wiped from Drummer's records, and no one can tell me why. Or rather, no one will. It was a mystery that kept me occupied for a time, but one I was forced to give up unsolved. I'd strongly suggest you do the same."

Kincaid could accept this. There were peculiarities about such things that he had come across before. Throughout man's history there were places, things, even people that became inadvisable to be associated with according to the group knowledge of a community or culture and the feeling persisted long after the actual cause was forgotten. People would simply think of the name of the thing and shudder, not even knowing why – only that it was the appropriate response.

Still, one half-answer was insufficient. "And the writing on the altar?"

Woolley sat down on a stump beside the road, still not meeting Kincaid's eye as they spoke. "I haven't seen it myself – it's just one of those things, as I've said. An elderly relative, a friend of a friend of a friend, something like that – people say they've seen it, but only when the light of a full moon falls on the altar. And there are other things besides, things far worse than writing no one can decipher."

A moment passed with each man left to his own thoughts. Kincaid broke the pause. "Wallace wanted to see for himself."

Woolley nodded. "Yes. But you already knew that."

Kincaid **had** known it; he supposed he'd known it from the moment he'd read Wallace's long-delayed letter.

And now, he had to see it for himself.

IV.

It was now well into the afternoon and, though tired from his morning's exertions and his poor sleep the night before, Kincaid had no time to waste. He was determined to view with his own eyes whatever wonders or terrors hovered about the altar in the hills and he knew that the moon would be, if not entirely full, then very nearly so that night. He hoped it would be enough as, if he had another option, he might have waited until the night legends said was optimal and the moon had achieved its full power, but the bus to Lancaster would arrive in the morning and he did not intend to stay in Drummer any longer than was absolutely necessary.

At his hotel, Kincaid filled one jacket pocket with his remaining snack supply and the other with his electric torch and the small, snub-nosed revolver which had lain tucked into the bottom of his valise before he moved swiftly out of the village and along the ill-kept road he'd traveled only hours earlier. Bathed in the sun's dying light, he made the trip rapidly up into the tree-covered hills, fueled by determination and aided by familiarity with the path.

The moon was a huge, silver disc that hung in the sky above the hills by the time Kincaid reached the point at which he'd have to climb and he shivered as the orb's weird light flooded open spaces with stark whiteness and etched shadows deeper than seemed natural. Kincaid's heart raced and he knew it was not simply from the physical activity – there was something in the air he could not identify. His rational mind urged him onward and upwards towards the top of the hill and the answers to the questions that burned his brain, but his soul screamed with a New Englander's superstition, long-repressed and asserting itself at last. It was a superstition hardwired into his very being, handed down from ancestors who'd made this land their own, but could never truly conquer it. He shook off the idea and began to climb.

The feeling only grew stronger the further he went. It told him this was no fit place for a man who wanted to keep his soul and sanity his own. Living in peace in Montville, a place so far from the heart of New England and so civilized it was practically removed from it altogether, Kincaid had been able to scoff at old fashioned ideas like north woods cults and things that go bump in the dark but here – here! – in these dark and eerily-lit woods, in a place as wild as could be found in these parts, he was not sure. As he achieved the top of the hill, he took a moment to center himself, preparing for whatever he was about to confront.

In the clearing where the altar stood, he was relieved to find nothing immediately out of place or suspicious, though the feeling of unease continued to grow, sending icy worms crawling through his guts. The altar itself, bathed in the silvery lunar glow, stood out boldly from its surroundings and as Kincaid made to study it, he was disturbed that his weary eyes seemed to find faint suggestions of weird etchings on the stone – marks that had not been present during his first visit. Whenever he became aware of them, however, and made to take close inspection – they were gone. Look away, and he'd swear he saw stone hieroglyphics glowing under the moonlight from out of the corner of his eye. Turn back – nothing.

Kincaid moved away, back to the edge of the clearing, and armed himself with his flashlight in one hand and his pistol in the other before sitting down and pulling his knees to his chest. Within him, emotions and rationality warred, but he knew he must get to the bottom of this thing even at the risk of danger to himself. He felt he owed that to Ted Wallace, though he couldn't have said why.

Alone in the woods, Kincaid questioned his own motives for the first time. Why did he owe Ted anything? This entire predicament was of Wallace's design, and Kincaid had gotten involved long after any real difference could be made. The line of reasoning surprised him – these were not Bertram Kincaid's thoughts. Bertram Kincaid and Theodore Wallace had been the best of friends and while it was true that they had inevitably grown apart some over the years, a man was nothing without loyalty. Questioning that was as alien to Kincaid as he was coming to believe this place was to the wholesome Earth he knew.

Whatever otherness existed in this glade, on top of this hill, surrounding this carved piece of rock that did not belong, was invading Kincaid in a way he would not have thought possible. He had always dismissed anything he could not see, could not touch, could not quantify, qualify and record in neat little books and ledgers. But in this place of evil repute and eerie mien, he knew he had been wrong – as Wallace had been wrong. These tales the villagers told were no superstitions repeated for generations by an ignorant people, but truths shared among those made wise by experience and wanting only to prevent what befell their own distant ancestors from befalling others. Kincaid grimaced and wondered if Wallace, too, had come to that conclusion.

Shaken from dark thoughts by a noise that was not natural to the forest, Kincaid's eyes flicked open and he realized that he must have dozed. His first sight was of the altar, glowing wickedly and proudly as if it had absorbed the day's light and was hurling it back out into the night for its own purposes. He leapt to his feet without conscious intention and moved closer, kneeling down and gazing this way and that, running his fingers lightly over the designs that were now prominently evident, but were not, indeed, carved into the stone itself. He had no idea what science or sorcery could make them appear under the light of the full moon, but the symbols that adorned the altar were clearly visible – arcane scribblings that resembled no earthly writing Kincaid knew of, but instead sent his thoughts hurtling back to those long-gone musings he'd shared with Wallace over the Mad Arab's book and the ghastly figures it contained which belonged to a people who were not men that had lived long before this area was even above the brine of an ancient sea.

So engrossed was he in his investigations that Kincaid did not notice he was no longer alone until a weird, haunting trilling piped by some unseen musician began to fill the area. He whirled, seeking its source, only to start in fright and crouch to press his back tightly against the altar for whatever measure of protection he could gain. The circumference of the little glade was ringed by robed figures, their faces lost in shadow but uniformly tall and moving silently save for whichever one was playing the unholy tune that filled the air.

The newcomers seemed to pay Kincaid no attention and linked hands, forming a circle around the entire clearing, broken only when one stepped forward from the group to approach the altar and the others immediately closed the circle again. Kincaid was sure the one moving slowly forward intended to confront him and wrenched free from the grip of fear to throw himself to one side and practically jump into a standing position. Remembering the pistol in his hand, he brandished it towards the hooded being and shouted, "Come no closer!"

The weird worshipper ignored him entirely, however, and kneeled before the altar, much as Kincaid himself had done earlier, though with far more reverence. The others around the glade began to sing in a wordless chant that mimicked the strange, increasingly frenetic piping that seemed to be coming from all around them. Kincaid was terrified but could do nothing save stand watching as the being threw back its hood, revealing a man a little older than Kincaid himself, whose already-racing heart pounded even harder as he saw a more-than-vague resemblance to his own features in the other's face!

Kincaid took a step back, realized that would only put him within reach of the other cultists, as he now thought of them, and resumed his former stance. He was trapped with no option but to see this thing out and hope for a chance of escape. Keeping his firearm trained on the man who shared his likeness, Kincaid watched.

As he did, the kneeler made signs of obeisance before the altar, his head tilted back and eyes closed, wearing a look of mixed ecstasy and anticipation. His movements were intricate and Kincaid found himself curiously intrigued, temporarily overcoming his terror. The man's rhythmic motions were echoed by the worshippers who ringed the glade and as the music continued to pick up intensity and tempo, so did their ritual gyrations. This continued for some moments before reaching a fever pitch, and Kincaid wondered how long they could possibly keep up this level of frenzy, until the crazily genuflecting man nearest the altar reached his climax and whipped his neck forward, slamming his head into the still-glowing altar, shocking Kincaid and bringing forth in him a new wave of horror and revulsion. The man crumpled to the ground, insensate or dead Kincaid could not tell, and the others changed their demoniac hymn, transitioning smoothly from high-pitched, frantic wailing to a low, slow, droning chant that did nothing to alleviate the terrified intruder's unease.

From either side of the clearing approached two of the robed figures who not only drew back their hoods, but shed their robes entirely as they moved closer to the altar, revealing themselves as male and female and making visible faces akin to both Kincaid's and the man he now realized was a willing sacrifice. Kincaid wondered if these two were also sacrifices, their naked bodies gleaming palely under the eerie light of the altar and the moon, when together they hefted the first victim's body onto the low platform and traced curious designs on their own breasts with the blood still flowing from their fellow's head-wound. They had not, to this point, joined in the low chanting of their peers, but now they turned towards one another, flung out their arms, linked hands, and began a tune of their own, one of faster tempo but even lower pitch. In unison, and still holding each other, they began to whirl and weave and twist their bodies this way and that, ever faster, until Kincaid feared they would repeat the suicidal act of the first man. He chanced a look at the other figures around the clearing and took note that they ignored the dancers just as they still ignored him. Instead, the empty-seeming hoods were all fixed on the altar itself and the body that lay upon it, pumping out its remaining life to spill across and cover the stone, which seemed to increase in luminance as the vulgarly twirling pair capered.

As the brilliance from the altar began to reach a point nearly equaling the noontime sun, the disparate chants of the main group and the single pair reached a sort of synchronicity until they were intoning the same words once again. Kincaid could at first understand none of it, but interspersed with various others, came again and again the words *"Iä! Iä! Yog-Sothoth! Yog-Sothoth fhtagn!"* and at their recognition from his scant studies in the occult, Kincaid was seized by a bone-deep terror that threatened to either break his wits or freeze his very breath in his lungs. The chanting grew exponentially intense until all voices coalesced into a single wordless shout of exultation as the evil piping reached its crescendo, and the dancers their finish, as blinding light, of a different cast than had been seen previously, burst forth from the altar to engulf the sacrifice only to fade instantly.

By sheer instinct, Kincaid had managed to throw up an arm to protect his eyes but even through his eyelids, arm and clothing, was still left with spots dancing across his vision. He blinked furiously, trying to clear it, and was rewarded with the sight that would remained seared into his nightmares for the rest of his days.

Draped repulsively across the altar, where the young man's body had been, was a great conglomeration of iridescent, pulsating globes and writhing tentacles which shone wetly in the light from the moon, now the only means of illumination but still far more than Kincaid wished. The thing was massive, easily the size of a small house, yet seemed to be confined somehow to an area only slightly greater than the dimensions of the altar and a height of a dozen or so feet above it. The measurements could not possibly add up, as if the thing was not only alien to nature but refused to obey its laws out of sheer contrariness. Kincaid's tormented mind took note of this as the thing sat wetly squirming and, all around the circle, its worshippers dropped to their knees chanting "*Iä! Yog-Sothoth!*" over and over, their previous hymns forgotten. Even the formerly-unseen piper came forth from the shadows, tossing his bone-white and eerily-glowing instrument away, to fall prostrate before the monstrous deity.

The dancers kneeled also, presenting themselves to the horror before them, which seemed to appraise the pair with many hideous eyes before lashing out with dozens of tentacles to ensnare the man and pull him into its own writhing mass. Kincaid could bear no more, turning away and retching as the damp slurping and noisome odor from the thing finally overcame his mental wards. An instant later, he broke into a run back towards the edge of the clearing he had originally come from.

No one moved to impede him as he rushed headlong through the trees, heedless of the branches slapping his face and tearing at his clothing or the loose stones threatening to trip him. Somewhere in his mind, he knew this was what Wallace had seen and done those many full moons ago and he would later envy his friend's apparent retreat into his own mind.

Kincaid ran faster, longer and harder than he had known he was capable of, and did not stop until he reached the home of Sherman Woolley. Not caring if he woke Woolley's neighbors as well, he pounded on the door and lower windows until a light went on inside and the door swung open to reveal the older man in shirt and nightcap, carrying an oil lamp and wearing a scowl.

"Are you mad?" he hissed. "Come inside!" Not waiting to see if Kincaid followed, Woolley made to head back inside, but Kincaid grabbed the man's sleeve, preventing his going.

"I may very well be!" Kincaid blurted out. "You must dress and come with me!"

Woolley jerked his arm away from Kincaid's grasp, his scowl deepening. "It's nearly four in the morning. I'm not going anywhere!"

Kincaid's tone softened and his face contorted into a mask of desperation. "Please," he said, barely above a whisper. "I've been to the altar again..."

"Good Lord!" Woolley cried. "You *are* insane!" He then demanded that Kincaid tell him of everything he'd witnessed, and the younger man promised to do so only if Woolley accompanied him back to the site on the hill. The former-teacher finally assented, his desire to hear those dark secrets outweighing his annoyance at being awakened or the inconvenience of an unplanned hike, and dressed quickly.

As they traveled, Kincaid told Woolley all that had occurred on the hill until the moment he fled, though he left out the goriest of details for propriety's sake. Woolley was thrilled to have at last an account from someone with firsthand knowledge, though he pressed Kincaid time and again on the issue of whether he had really experienced what he saw or if it had merely been some intensely vivid dream. Kincaid admitted that he believed he had dozed for a time, but insisted that what he saw was real.

They arrived on the hill as the sun was just beginning its climb across the heavens and, both of them eager to be done with the thing one way or the other, climbed swiftly to the top. Woolley had never been to the altar personally, but tried to quell his excitement out of respect for what Kincaid believed had happened to him. In the clearing, none of the sinisterness of the night before was evident and Woolley dryly remarked on what a lovely morning it was shaping up to be.

For his part, Kincaid was relieved – despite the absolute reality it had seemed in the night, the chain of events he'd experienced must have been an insane dream after all. When Woolley wanted to examine the altar itself more closely, Kincaid agreed, now much lighter of heart than he had felt he'd ever be again. They looked the thing up and down, peering curiously and closely at its every surface, but there was no sign of the markings Kincaid had seen nor the blood stains that were to be expected, had any ritual taken place here mere hours earlier. Woolley seemed quite disappointed, but Kincaid was elated.

Together, the two men walked back towards Drummer. Woolley attempted to converse further about Kincaid's dream, as he now knew it to be, but the younger man would have none of it – it was something best left in the realm of the night, a figment born of time spent in a strange place at an unusual hour and fueled by the murmurings of the unknown. He preferred, instead, to enjoy the beautiful day that was unfolding around them. Woolley was not entirely convinced, however, and declared his intention to investigate the site further – to which Kincaid smiled and sincerely wished him luck.

Near Woolley's house, Kincaid thanked his new friend for the assistance and support provided during his short stay in Drummer and the pair pledged to keep in contact. Woolley also promised to provide updates on Ted Wallace as much as possible, for which Kincaid was grateful. A hearty handshake and more words of well-wishing followed then they separated as their paths diverged – Woolley to his home and Kincaid off to collect his belongings before boarding the bus that would return him to Lancaster and the swiftest path back towards the civilization he knew.

V.

The bus was exactly on time; Kincaid boarded and passed his quarter fare to the driver, who inquired about his stay in Drummer. With a smile, Kincaid replied that it was an interesting place to visit, but he could not imagine wanting to live there. The driver nodded uncomprehendingly and put the vehicle into motion, leaving Kincaid to take his pick of the mostly-empty seats.

The journey home was entirely uneventful, for which Kincaid was thankful, and by Monday afternoon he was walking the dusty road from Montville proper to his sorely-missed home. He had spent the previous days' travel time ruminating on all that had occurred during his sojourn and lamenting the fate that had struck down poor Ted Wallace. He believed he understood now what had happened to his friend, but still could not entirely explain it. It was clear that there was something unknown and unusual about the altar, and that area in general, but presented with no clear evidence of real, physical happenings he knew he must concede that what he, and presumably Wallace, had seen was entirely in their own heads.

The mind was powerful, there was no doubt, and the absolute conviction with which the people of Drummer believed the tales they told had a kind of power of its own. Kincaid chuckled at his own temporary reversal of opinion in those night-haunted woods, utterly taken in by the things he had been told, and by what he had seen of the town, when his brain had assembled all of the pieces in the way that he must have subconsciously *wanted* them to be. In the darkness, under the stars, mired in drowsiness and exhaustion, the puzzle had fit together perfectly and horribly and Kincaid had no other choice but to believe in things that evaporated under cleansing daylight. Surely for Wallace, being much more deeply entrenched in the legends and lore of the region and therefore arguably more susceptible to their influence, such a process must have been infinitely stronger – only poor Ted never had the chance to once again see things in the pure light of day.

Upon returning to Montville, Kincaid endeavored to settle once again to his accustomed routines, throwing himself into the work commissioned by William Hillhouse, interrupted by the previous week's events, and hoping to transition smoothly back to his everyday life. In one sense he was successful, as the Hillhouse genealogy was completed swiftly and greeted with great satisfaction by the client. In others, however, he failed utterly. Try though he might, he could not entirely put out of his mind the gruesome images he had seen in Drummer – whether real or not – and his sleep was plagued by nightmares as vivid as his dream on the hill, while his daytime thoughts continued to wander back to those ghastly, phantom devotees whose faith and deity had nearly shattered Kincaid's sanity, as whatever images Wallace had seen had shattered his.

Time marched on and Kincaid coped as best he could; though it was obvious to others that something was wrong, he continued to deny it to himself in an effort to make it true. He spoke very little about his trip and before long, his friends and colleagues ceased asking, which made it easier for him to compartmentalize the events and lock them away. As such, he continued to function in a mostly-normal capacity and it was assumed by all, Kincaid included, that whatever was amiss would work itself out in its due course.

In the fourth week of July, Kincaid received a package wrapped in plain, brown paper and postmarked Lancaster, New Hampshire. Though there was no return address, he knew it had to have originated with Sherman Woolley and he was surprised to hear from the older man so soon. As they had agreed to keep in contact, particularly regarding the continued welfare of Ted Wallace, Kincaid felt a pang of fear at the thought that something further had happened to his friend, especially so quickly after Kincaid's visit.

He unwrapped the parcel to find it contained a letter and a second, smaller package, also sheathed in brown paper. The interior bundle was oblong and about the length of a man's forearm; Kincaid put it aside for the moment and perused the letter, which read:

July 16th, 1923

Dear Mr. Kincaid –

I trust you've returned home and to your life safely and satisfactorily and that this letter finds you exceedingly well. I suppose you had not expected to hear from me this soon and truthfully, I did not expect to have cause to write.

I imagine you will assume the worst upon receiving this but rest assured, to the best of my knowledge, your friend Mr. Wallace is still in as good a state of health as is possible. As promised, I have visited Mrs. Powell's home weekly since your departure and, though she resents the intrusion, I know Mrs.

Powell appreciates the concern you showed for her adopted "son".

To the purpose of this letter, however — you will recall my plans to continue the investigations into our local mystery. While I have had very little luck in gaining additional information from any of the townsfolk, I have made extensive study of the altar itself and the area surrounding it and found a few things of interest, though none as striking as the visions you related to me.

Inspired by Mr. Wallace's work and your own findings, I have decided to write a detailed history of Drummer and its own peculiar mythology. As I recall you are a writer and historian yourself, I would like to collaborate with you on this venture, at least to the extent of having you audit the body of evidence I have unearthed and perhaps editing drafts of the work when they are ready.

If you are not interested, I will understand and will take no offense as I realize that your visit to Drummer was hardly a pleasant one and that you may not wish to be reminded further of it. Before you make any decision, however, I ask that you at least examine the artifact I have included with this missive. I discovered it near the clearing where the altar resides, the day after your departure. It is, to date, the only thing I have found at the site other than the altar itself, but I think you will agree it is most compelling.

Whether you choose to write in return or not, I ask that you please post the enclosed item back to me and have included sufficient funds to do so. I look forward to hearing from you.

Sincerely,

Kincaid's brow furrowed as he read the letter. The fact that Wallace was, at least of its writing, still in relatively good health was welcome news but Woolley's opening up of a scarcely-closed psychic wound was troubling. He knew the man had no intention of doing any harm but wished that Woolley had waited at least a while longer before trying to re-engage Kincaid regarding the ordeal that still plagued his sleep.

Still, he was curious as to what his northerly friend had discovered and hefted the smaller package from its resting spot on his desk. The wrapped object was not heavy and as he tore away the paper gently, for fear of damaging the thing, he became aware of a queasy feeling in his belly similar to that he'd experienced on that far away hill amidst untouched greenery.

As Kincaid peeled away the final layer, a shriek rose unbidden in his throat and he dropped the thing as if it were venomous. It crashed unceremoniously to the floor of his study where it lay, rocking gently back and forth, impelled by the momentum of its fall – a stark-white recorder, made of bone or ivory, and carved with queerly pigmented markings identical to those he had seen on the altar in the hills under the light of a full New England moon.

Suck It Up,
Get It Done

Cement dust rained across my feet as I whacked my hammer into the crumbling wall where Marty, my supervisor, figured the blockage was and wondered how long it'd been since anyone "maintained" this area.

I'd been working sewer maintenance for the city of Boston about four months, but I was just now realizing there were literally miles of tunnels, even in the little territory of the old North End I'd been assigned. I doubted anyone had visited this one recently and it showed in the decaying walls and walkways.

I know you're thinking "the sewer? Sick!" but it's not that bad – especially considering my prospects were pretty limited. I'm twenty-two so you'd think I'd have options, right? But all I got's a GED and a pregnant girlfriend and this is a good job. It's union and pays well – just gotta suck it up and get it done.

I took another swing at the wall hiding the pipe I needed to inspect and howled a little in surprise when the whole thing came tumbling down, throwing me off balance so I fell forward into the tunnel on the other side. Choking on dust and wiping my watering eyes, I thought *Marty's gonna shit a brick* when a wet hissing sound – sorta like when you blow into a straw after your cup is empty – hit my ears. I nearly shit one myself, thinking I'd broken the pipe I was there to unclog.

My eyes were still stinging but I had to check the damage before getting Marty over here, so at least he couldn't say I didn't own up to it, and aimed my flashlight towards the sound. Man, I wish I hadn't! I screamed and dropped my light, but fear of screwing up beat fear of what was in front of me cuz I picked it right back up and looked again.

The pipe was blocked, alright – by a hissing, stinking thing that reminded me of a little kid werewolf with mange. Its lower half was wedged in the pipe, but its upper half was piss-yellow and brown, hissing, wriggling desperately and swiping at me with unnaturally-long fingers ending in filthy-looking claws. It shrieked when I shone the light directly on it and I saw big, black eyes snap closed in a face more dog than human. I almost felt bad.

I called Marty on my walkie; he was pissed I interrupted lunch, but I said I had something I didn't know how to handle. He asked if it could wait, I said probably not. He showed up fifteen minutes later, took a look in the hole, swore a little then said I'd done the right thing. He didn't seem surprised or nothing, just annoyed.

I was glad *someone* was calm, cuz *I* was close to freaking out. Here was this… *demon* or something in the damned sewer! I asked if I should call the cops, but Marty gave me a sneer and, rummaging in his big toolbox, said, "We ain't bothering them. This is just part of the job."

"Part of the job?!" I'd signed on to fix pipes and stuff, not deal with monsters.

My eyes went wide as Marty pulled a big revolver from his box and handed it to me with a hard look. I took it, but said I didn't know anything about guns. "What's to know?" he asked. "Point and shoot."

I'd had enough, and said so. Even the new guy needs an idea of what's going on. Marty actually seemed sympathetic, for once, and patted my shoulder. "Look, Sean," he pointed towards the little squirmy thing still in the pipe. "That's a ghoul – just a lil' baby one, of course. These hills used to be chock full of 'em and they'd run all around under the city. You'd hear about 'em sometimes. Not much anymore, but once in a while you find one. They break into the pipes, looking for food I guess, and like it or not, anything that happens down here is part of our job. So – take care of it. Okay?"

I nodded, slowly. It did sort of make sense, even though I didn't like it. I aimed at the critter and fired, the sound so loud in that little space you'd swear the roof would cave in. Marty hadn't lied – it was easy, though the kickback made my elbow sore. He helped me pull the thing from the pipe, patch up the holes it'd made and recap it.

When we were done, he packed up his toolbox but as I tried to give him the gun he put up a hand and said, "Nah, you're gonna need it."

I must have looked at him funny cuz he pointed into the darkened tunnel and said, "Babies got mommas don't they, dumbass?"

I sighed. *Suck it up. Get it done.*

The Thing
that
Remained

I'm not mad, I tell you! There's evidence to prove what I say is true – you saw it yourselves! Right there in my own house, in my own guest bedroom – which I opened out of a sense of charity and decency, mind you; I didn't have to – exactly as I found it this morning. I didn't touch a thing, and I'll swear it on anything you ask me to. Besides, what *man* could *do* such a thing!? Certainly not I – look at me! I'm no lay about and I stay in decent shape, but I'm no strongman. You'd need a simply *unnatural* amount of strength to do what was done to poor Olcott and anyway how do you account for the–

What?

Alright, yes. Yes! I'll try to calm down. Yes, thank you, a cigarette would be wonderful just now.

Again? But I've already – oh, hello, Chief Constable. Yes, if it'll put this thing to rest, if you'll finally believe me, I'll tell you the story, too.

Let me start me by saying I am no archaeologist, pathfinder or even plain tomb raider, just so we are clear from the outset. I do consider myself an explorer, however, and am acquainted with a number of those in the aforementioned fields – but I myself confine my studies to the wealth of data such professionals accumulate. I do this not as an occupation, though I have had such successes as to bring me some small renown in certain circles. The station to which I was born allows me the freedom to pursue my avocation, and I am overall quite satisfied with my lot.

Taking this into account, I was more than a bit surprised when I received the telegram from Rudolph Olcott. It read simply:

YOUR ASSISTANCE REQUIRED. HANDSOME PAY. WILL ARRIVE ON 5TH MAY.

It being the afternoon of the fourth, I was somewhat vexed. Even having not spoken to him in years, this seemed typical of the man. It was exactly like Olcott to assume his needs outweighed whatever plans I may have had. I have to admit, however, that the content of the message intrigued me.

I had once considered Olcott a colleague, in the broadest sense of the word, but his cutthroat attitude towards scientific and academic achievement left a sour taste in my mouth. For Olcott, the glory of a new discovery or triumph far outweighed the thing itself and his desires were geared towards merely his own betterment, rather than those of mankind as a whole. There was no denying his skills or talent, though; as much of a glory hound as he was, none of his accomplishments were unearned. If he was demanding my assistance he must be onto something extraordinary, indeed.

While men like Olcott travel the globe hunting forgotten treasures in hidden tombs and ruins, I prefer to remain safely in my little home here in Arkham, studying the things they bring back. I have no specific qualifications, no official training per se, but I have made it my life's work to unlock the secrets left behind in words few living men can read. My delight is the myriad scraps of scrollwork, fragments of tablets, even photographs and rubbings from crumbling walls the world over which adventurers of all stripes bring back with them. In that capacity, I have made some few, small breakthroughs – enough that the name Elwood

Upton would be recognized by those who share my passion.

I spent the rest of that afternoon tidying up for my expected company and mentally running through various scenarios which would bring Olcott rushing to my doorstep.

The fifth dawned wet and dreary, and so I forwent my accustomed morning stroll to the café on Garrison Street for breakfast. I also had no inkling of when Olcott might arrive and, as much as I disliked the man, I would be a very poor host indeed to leave him waiting in the rain for my return. I made a pot of coffee and some toast and occupied myself with the previous day's half-read newspaper.

Shortly before three o'clock, a frantic knocking on my door drove me from the comfort of my den, thoughts racing at the urgency it conveyed. It must be Olcott, I knew, but I couldn't fathom what nervous energy could impel such frenetic rapping or what it portended. God, how I wish I'd never opened that door!

But open it I did, to find Olcott standing huddled and soaking wet on my flagstones. I quickly ushered him inside, took his sopping greatcoat and woolen muffler and tried to take the small canvas knapsack slung over his shoulder, as well, but he would not part with it. Then I ushered him into the den, seating him in my own chair by the fire, before hurrying to find a towel. All the while, Olcott said not a word, but accepted my assistance mutely. When he was as settled as I could make him, I pulled up a chair beside his and asked if he had walked all the way from the other side of town in this storm and why, if so.

Olcott started, as if just becoming aware he was not alone, and stared out of sunken, haunted eyes at me, causing me to shrink back unconsciously. I could scarcely believe that this was the same hearty adventurer I'd known, in years past, to bluster and boast his way through any occasion. Olcott's features were recognizable, but only just; he'd lost the vitality and boldness that had characterized him, and they had been replaced with an air of sickliness and timidity that was palpable. His hair had gone gray and his skin, once bronzed from tramping around sun-soaked climes, had a pallor I did not associate with the living. I couldn't imagine what had effected such a change.

The man looked around with quick, darting turns of his head and constantly roaming eyes and, after a moment, appeared to have satisfied himself that there was no danger, for he visibly relaxed. Not entirely, but enough to converse rationally, at least. He turned towards me, a weak half-smile on his lips, and said in a raspy voice barely more than a whisper, "Thank you for seeing me, El. I know we haven't always been cordial to each other, but I knew you wouldn't turn me down. You're just too damned decent."

His use of such an address, when previously we'd simply been "Upton" and "Olcott" to one another, was yet another oddity but I nodded, unsure of what else to do, and repeated my earlier question.

"Yes, I walked here. I couldn't find a taxicab and I doubt one would have taken me, anyway. At least not the whole way here."

I didn't understand and said so. When Olcott didn't reply after several minutes, I stood and declared my intention to make a fresh pot of coffee to warm the both of us up. Before I could take a step, however,

Olcott's hand shot out and latched onto my wrist with a strength I wouldn't have believed the emaciated form still possessed, preventing my leaving. I looked at the man, stunned, as he slowly released his grip, and asked me not to leave him alone.

Assenting, I sat back down and said, "Well, then, at least tell me what this is about."

Olcott took a deep breath that ended in a hacking cough, but waved me off when I made to help by patting him on the back. "I'm alright, I'm alright," he assured me, though his tortured-sounding lungs suggested otherwise. He cleared his throat for some time before continuing, but his voice was stronger than it had been when he did. "Look, El, I'm sorry to have come here without any real notice and I'm sorry to drag you into this, but I don't know to whom else I can turn. I won't lie, you're not the first person I've been to, but your name kept coming up and it became obvious I had no choice. I'm hoping you'll let bygones be bygones and at least try to help. And I meant what I said in that telegram – I'll pay you any price you can name if you're successful."

I told him I'd do my best, but that he still hadn't explained what was going on and that I must know that before I agreed to anything. Olcott nodded, coughed a time or two and said, "I know I'm being vague, but I swear, it's for your own sake. Some of the details… it's best I don't share them. But I wouldn't ask you the favor I'm going to without giving you some idea as to why, so I'll try to give you the broad strokes without filling in any details you don't need.

"You know what I'm about – all too well, I suppose, since it's chiefly been the cause of whatever strife has existed between us in the past. I won't apologize for that, I've lived my life the way I wanted to, same as anyone else. It has lead me to my current predicament, though, so maybe there's something to be said for your reservations – but, anyway…

"About three years ago, I was dining at the Explorer's Club in New York when Horatio Sandring, don't know if you've heard of him, approached and asked if he might join me. I was reluctant, as the man's not exactly top shelf and has a bit of a reputation as a fibber, but I relented so as not to make a scene. I expected him to try and regale me with some wild tale spun from whole cloth, but instead, he got rather conspiratorial and first made me swear to tell no one what he was about to share with me. It was an easy promise to make as I had no intention, at the time, of spreading any of his little stories. Now, I almost wish I hadn't, but I am a man of my word, so I won't. Suffice it to say, it involved a ruin Sandring had somehow discovered, but hadn't the courage to explore beyond a bit of poking around the surface. It had the sound of truth to it, with details I doubt he has the imagination to concoct and I was intrigued. I wrung the location of it from him: deep in a hidden valley in Indochina.

"Circumstances prevented me from using the information until last year, however. It had been some time since I'd sojourned in the Orient, but my contacts were still good and putting together an expedition wasn't much of a chore. The trip in was fairly uneventful – I found the place relatively easily with Sandring's directions and it was much as he'd described, though it was located in a very out-of-the-way place that I doubt any white man has much explored; I've yet to find it named on any map. The local porters I'd hired got nervous as we entered the valley, but they forged ahead with some prodding. The ruin itself was built into the living stone of a small mountain, about a third of the way up, and was of an architectural sort that doesn't correspond to anything I've ever seen of Oriental building of any known people. I could not even begin to guess its age. The façade had crumbled, but the entrance was not hard to find, it still being open from when Sandring had dug it out, and the interior seemed quite sound.

"There was a main chamber, dominated by a kind of circular platform that was too big to be an altar, but might have once held some sort of ceremonial kit. Branching off from that room, there were six small side chambers and a long corridor leading deeper into the mountain itself. A quick search of the side chambers revealed nothing of interest. The final corridor was blocked off only a short ways in by a heavy door sporting intricate ornamentation which struck me as vaguely sinister, and a kind of stone mechanism very much like a bank vault's dial. Sandring hadn't mentioned this, and it amused me to think that in his cowardice he hadn't even come this far. What, after all, is the point of adventuring if you're too fearful to take chances? But I digress.

"That great, stone lock gave me some trouble, despite its age and relative simplicity. I kept listening for tumblers, but could hear none. I've still no idea how I managed, but after a few hours of messing about with it, I got the thing open. When I did, a gust of insufferably-rank wind almost knocked me over, blowing out of the blackness from that timeless vault. My native hands, who had been milling around restlessly all the while I worked, finally broke and ran then. The two white men who'd come with me, an

Englishman who resides in Hong Kong and a Frenchman born in the colony, urged me not to proceed any further. The locals had good instincts, they said, and if they would not go on, neither should we. I dismissed this as foolishness, of course, and to their credit the men abided by my decision.

"We ventured down into the tunnel, covering our mouths and noses to avoid the worst of the stench, and lighting our way with electric torches. We must have marched through the darkness for a good mile or more, the whole way past strings of nonsense symbols like I'd never seen carved into the walls and I found them interesting enough to have taken a few sheets of charcoal rubbings for later study. Eventually, we came to a chamber about half the size of the main one. We searched it all around, but other than a huge, circular stone slab in the center, there was nothing – no treasure, no artifacts, no way to continue on. The stench had grown all the more powerful the deeper we went and I realized immediately it was coming from beneath that mammoth stone disc. Again against the wishes of my men, I decided we had to have it up; I hadn't come this far for nothing. At this they balked and no amount of threatening or cajoling would change the Frenchman's mind, but my faithful Englishman helped me lever it aside after retrieving our tools."

Olcott's story was cut off by a choking fit that seemed to wrack his entire body. The strain of so much talking was becoming evident. I, however, was literally on the edge of my seat. I had heard many of his tales in the past, but this seemed to have none of the boastful exaggerations of his others. I doubt I could have been more excited had I actually been in that far-off pit of darkness. I waited until he got himself back under control and urged him to continue.

He began again, a bit unsteadily at first, but quickly regaining his momentum. "So, we levered the thing aside, surprised at its relative lightness compared to its size, only to face further disappointment – there was nothing inside. The hole it covered was not deep, perhaps three and a half feet, but the smell was positively nauseating. My companion stated that he was leaving and I could join him or not, but he could not stand the smell any longer. I relented and followed, bitterly cursing the fact that Sandring's instincts had been correct, probably for the first time in his life.

"In the more wholesome air of the outer chamber, the smell was much dissipated, but still present. To this, we attributed a clinging quality and changed our clothes before gathering as much gear as the two of us could carry and setting back out. Despite vigorous washing at the earliest opportunity, the smell continued to haunt us throughout our return trip through the jungle – sometimes faint and sometimes strong, but always present.

"Back in civilization, we parted ways, and I decided to take a brief vacation in Europe before heading back home. Only a few days into my sea voyage, however, the clean scent of the salt and spray began to take a backseat to that noisome one I thought I'd left behind in the jungle. I'd had whiffs of it before then, but I had thought these a sort of sense memory. That was clearly not the case, however, when crew and other passengers of the liner I was aboard began to comment. It wasn't much longer before I was put off the ship, left to find my own way.

"Everywhere I went it was the same. It was a long, hard trip overland until I finally reached the relative-modernity of Asia Minor and could take a train the remainder of my journey to the French coast. The whole way there, however, that damnable stench followed and before long... things began to happen."

I shook my head in puzzlement, but did not interrupt, hoping he would elaborate. I was not disappointed.

"I know how that sounds, but I swear it is no figment of the mind. By the nature of my travels, I was moving nearly constantly, striving to return to the environs I knew. When I stopped for more than a night or two, at most, the smell would grow very strong and it would be accompanied by doings that could not be explained. It started with sounds in the night – sibilant whisperings with no discernible source or the rattling of windows as if something attempted entry. If I moved on, the stench subsided, as if I left it behind me, though it never quite disappeared, and the sounds would mostly stop.

"Then one night, shortly after I crossed the border into Turkey, I twisted an ankle after tumbling over a stone in the dark and cracked my head. I awoke in the home of a farmer who had found and taken me in. He explained that I had been senseless the whole previous night and most of the day. The stench was nearly overpowering; the farmer made no comment on it, but I apologized nonetheless and made to excuse myself, thanking him for his hospitality, only to discover that my ankle was in no fit state to support me, much less carry me the distance I needed it to. The man was most gracious, especially to a stranger; he refused to let me leave and offered his home for as long as I needed it.

He said he, too, had once been on hard times and he understood my plight." Olcott laughed bitterly at this, surprising me, before continuing. "It was kind of him, and I am thankful, but he paid the price for that kindness in a way I can never repay.

"Loathe as I was to remain, it seemed I had no choice and consented to one more night. The farmer seemed pleased, and he and his wife bandaged my ankle and prepared me a simple meal. They offered me a bath, perhaps making a subtle judgment on the smell they must have assumed came from my body, but I declined and instead went back to bed, falling into an uneasy sleep.

"That night, I was awakened by the clattering shutters of the little farmhouse and a noxiousness so strong it brought tears to my eyes. The building was only two rooms, and I wondered how the farmer and his wife were able to continue sleeping; if the noise had not awakened them, surely the smell must have. I crept from my bed and to the flimsy door that separated the halves of the building, opening it as quietly and cautiously as possible. A fetid wind identical to that in a far-off Oriental jungle assaulted my senses and blew the door wide open, nearly colliding with me, and revealing the answer to my questions – by the moonlight streaming in from the now-unshuttered windows, I saw that the poor souls who had taken pity on a helpless wanderer were dead, their devastated bodies smashed against the thin straw mattress which they slumbered upon after giving me their own bed's use, and dripping with a rank, yellowish ichor.

"In that moment, my mind broke – I fled the place in a senseless terror which did not dissipate until I was halfway to the city of Ankara, where I finally boarded a train bound for Europe a week later, with no memories between that instant and that of my grisly discovery. Had I not elected to sleep fully clothed, even continuing to wear my rucksack due to my almost-constant movement over the previous weeks, I would have been left with nothing at all – such was my single-minded determination to simply get away from that place as quickly as possible.

"The train trip was long and I had ample time to reflect on the past and present. I had suspected since before leaving Indochina that the ancient vault I had broken the seal of had not been meant to foil and keep intruders out, but rather to keep something *in*. The signs had been there nearly from the start and I, blind, heedless fool that I am, had blundered into something I could not understand and had unleashed horror on the world. The Turks were the first victims I had seen with my own eyes, but who knew how many dead had been left in my path? The idea ate at my soul and since then I haven't stayed in one place for more than a few hours, in terror at what might befall those around me."

Here, Olcott went silent again for several minutes, seemingly lost in his troubled thoughts. During this time I, too, took a moment to reflect on his story and the utterly insane nature of the things he had told me. Insane, yes, but true, I feared. His had none of the zeal that characterizes a madman's tale, merely a deep and abiding regret over his actions.

My guest was by this time thoroughly warm and dry and, since he had paused in his recitation, I stood to retrieve some sort of refreshment for the both of us, the time being well past when I normally had my supper, and figuring Olcott could surely do with nourishment. As I did so, I caught the faintest whiff of something unusual in the air. It was nothing definite, however, and I chalked it up as my overactive imagination buying too deeply into Olcott's story, true or not. As I made to leave, Olcott seemed reluctant to part company even for a few minutes, but I assured him he was quite safe and after some gentle coaxing he consented, though unhappily.

When I returned with bowls of reheated, leftover soup from the day before, Olcott was visibly agitated, having resumed the fidgeting, hyper-vigilant manner he'd possessed upon his arrival that afternoon. It took a fair while before he regained his composure, during which I encouraged him to relax, eat and finish his tale whenever he was ready. When he had put himself together again, Olcott apologized then favored me with a shadow of his old self, flashing a wry grin and complimenting me on my bedside manner. "You should have been a physician. You've missed your calling, it seems."

I dismissed his jest and again asked him to finish his story, if he was able – in response Olcott took a sip of soup, set down his bowl and glared into the fireplace, as if it had somehow offended him. He released a long sigh. "Rather I should show you, I suppose," and so saying, opened his satchel to draw forth a small ivory tube, such as maps are stored in.

"I don't blame you for doubting my tale. It is a mad one, and I well know it. You've been kinder than I probably deserve but I will impose on you at least this once more, El." Olcott uncapped the tube, drew from it three sheets of paper and spread them flat on the table nearby, weighing down the corners with our bowls. He beckoned me closer and asked, "What do you make of these?"

I gazed with amazement at the papers – they were charcoal rubbings, as Olcott had described having taken in that noisome corridor in a forgotten temple of an unknown people. I had already been inclined to believe the man, but here was tangible proof! Some might scoff, claiming such "proof" easy to fake, but combined with what I had heard and what I had observed of Olcott's condition, I chose to believe.

The room was dark and while the fire's illumination had been sufficient for talking, I needed more for study and brought over the lamp from the corner of the room. Such a thing could hardly shed light on what I saw, however. The rubbings were fainter than I would have liked, obviously made hastily, but I could discern hieroglyphics of a sort in neat, orderly rows of three upon three. They resembled nothing I could think of offhand and said so.

Olcott sagged as though someone had let the wind out of him. "I feared as much. I'm no linguist or paleographer, but I had hoped you might be familiar with whatever this is. Once I was home, I sought out every expert I could find who was willing to speak with me and all were helpless. But every one of them had the same advice– if any man can decipher this, it is Elwood Upton. And decipher it you must, El. I fear you're my last resort and my only hope of salvation."

The compliment was appreciated, but I was puzzled. "Why is decipherment so important?" The moment I said it, I suspected, but I allowed Olcott to speak for himself.

"It is my only clue," here he collapsed back into a chair, and held his head; I knew he was suppressing sobs, though whether of frustration or anguish or fear, I could not tell. After a moment, he again met my gaze and said, "I have awakened something that should not be. Something lying in wait for terrible freedom denied it by better men than myself. I don't know who built that temple, but they knew how to capture this… thing, whatever it may be. I should never have opened that tomb, but I did and now, I must find a way to contain this horror. I'll go back to that jungle, if I must, but I hope it won't come to that. *Please*, I need to know how it was first trapped and how I can do so again." At this, Olcott was once more overcome by emotion, and I turned away to allow him a measure of privacy.

When the breathing behind me had resumed a more normal rhythm, I sat down next to Olcott, placed a hand on his shoulder and promised to do my utmost. I cautioned him, however, that it would take time – I was no more familiar with these strange markings than he, and even if I were to decode their message with the aid of the materials I had at hand, there was no guarantee the answer he sought would be there. He nodded in understanding and thanked me more than was necessary.

It had grown very late, and I suggested that Olcott get some rest. He protested, stating that he preferred to help me work in any capacity he was able, but I assured him that while I would begin immediately he was of no use to me in his current state and I did not expect to make much progress that night, anyway. Confronted with logic that he could not refute, Olcott allowed me to show him to the guest bedroom on the second floor and thanked me again.

As I made my way back downstairs towards the den, I passed the coatrack on which my guest's coat and scarf rested and was struck by a foul odor that seemed almost a tangible thing. I took a hesitant whiff of

Olcott's clothing, not yet dry, and determined that they must be washed first thing in the morning, to be cleansed of the residue Olcott had seemingly carried with him, before heading back to my den and the task before me.

I gathered the most arcane books in my possession, including a copy of the rather badly-translated English edition of d'Erlette's *Cultes de Ghoules,* in which I'd thought I may have seen something with a vague kinship to the symbols before me. As I pored over the various tomes, I felt myself drowsing. The mantle clock showed that it was nearly midnight and though my mind raced, my body was fighting to maintain its pace.

I did drop off at some point and was roused later by a peculiar thumping sound from above me, which startled me for a moment until I remembered that I had a guest unfamiliar with the layout of my home, who had probably simply stumbled into a piece of furniture in the darkness. Making no attempt to continue working, I instead settled into my comfortable easy chair, recently occupied by Olcott. As I drifted back to sleep, the foul odor I had detected on the drying coat and scarf seeped into my nostrils, but my drowsy mind associated it with Olcott having rested in the chair for so many hours and I determined to give it a cleaning on the morrow.

The next morning, I awoke tolerably rested, considering I had forgone the use of my bed, and set about making a suitable breakfast for myself and Olcott. The stench I had encountered in the night was absent, even from Olcott's now-dry outerwear, and I smiled at my own imagination's conjuring; surely if such an odiousness had existed a few short hours before, it could not have dissipated so thoroughly on its own, and I convinced myself it was merely a figment of the mind.

As the savory aromas of eggs and ham filled the kitchen, I put the coffee pot on the stove and went upstairs to wake my guest and invite him down to eat. Partway up the stairs, though, I encountered again the hideous scent, now a definite reality, and began to worry that Olcott's visit might irrevocably alter the milieu of my home, as he seemed to carry it on his body. Before I had reached the end of the hallway where the spare bedroom lay, the smell was so bad I had to cover my nose with my sleeve. As I approached, my pace slowed involuntarily and I was suddenly filled with a terror I could not account for, as if the foulness in the air had managed to permeate my very soul.

The door to Olcott's room was still closed; when he did not answer my knocking, I called out several times, but still received no response. Continuing to protect my nose, my free hand trembled as I reached to turn the knob. The door was not locked, but I hesitated halfway through the turning and listened intently for any sounds of stirring within. When the silence remained unbroken, I steeled myself and pushed open the portal.

I was greeted by a foulness so overpowering, I was literally knocked senseless and woke later gasping with nausea, my head aching fiercely. I realized immediately, however, that the stench had mostly-vanished and was now only faintly detectable once again. As I had fallen outside of the room in my faint, I once more gathered my nerves to enter.

When I did, I saw that the place was relatively untouched beyond an open window and what Olcott himself had disturbed in his preparation for sleep. That is, until my eyes were drawn to the bed and the man himself, crushed into the mattress, eyes bulging in horror and covered in a thick, yellow ooze at the sight of which I again fainted dead away.

Seeker
in the
Dark

Darkness and terror amplified the sounds of my lungs and heart as I pressed myself between musty clothing.

Outside the door, the distinctive shuffle-click-shuffle-click footsteps grew nearer and I became aware of snuffling sounds as if it searched for scent, like a common cur.

Inevitably, it came to my hiding spot and great gusts of fetid breath blasted beneath the closet door. Having no inkling of its form, my imagination conjured up a black, dog-headed monstrosity.

Suddenly, the age-weakened wood jumped... but held. Another moment and the unique tread moved on.

Did I remain undetected? Or did it toy with me...?

Perchance

a

Dream

The darkest day of my life is painted in the sullen gray of mundane sameness and the swirling blacks of impotent rage. It is the day when the petty miseries that we all endure have grown into dreadful enormities and the truly awful incidents – those that no one should experience – come harder and faster than I know how to manage. By their weight I am broken.

It's not a sudden thing, not a matter of simply being unable to process one atrocious period or event, but the culmination of a lifetime's struggle. True, it is not a long lifetime, and perhaps things will still turn out for the best, but in a decisive moment I am determined to leave it all behind in search of something else. Whether that something is better or worse makes no difference at this junction, as long as it is unfamiliar. Surely some would call it a coward's choice, abandoning what passes for the existence I have built, and that may be, but I am not concerned with the opinions of others; I have never been and now is not the time to start.

Saying no goodbyes and wasting no time, I leave behind the edifice I call home and choose at random a direction in which to travel. I carry nothing, for I need nothing except a desire to find some measure of the freedom that I long for so painfully. I have worried, in the past, about the state of my mind and the structure of my soul, but my body... my body has always been the most reliable aspect of my being. I know that I can trust my own sturdy legs and so I do, allowing them to propel me to whatever terminus for which I am destined and allowing myself to revel in the Zen of motion, to lose conscious thought to the workings of the exquisite machine that is the human form. Even in my abject state, certain wonders are not lost on me.

So I walk and for the duration of a seemingly endless moment, I have captured a portion of the peace I yearn for. It is not to last, however, for something interrupts my journey, ripping me from my fragile tranquility and the irradiate refuge that I have briefly found. Reluctantly, I open eyes I didn't realize were closed and squint against the tremendous brightness in which I am bathed, the source of which I cannot imagine in my drowsy confusion.

I find that I am stark naked, my skin blistered and cracking under the ferocious gaze of a sun more intense than it has a right to be as it blazes down upon a region utterly foreign to my eyes. Suddenly fully awakened from my strange fugue, I realize that even now my legs have not ceased to propel me forward through this unknown place. I had placed my trust in them, and it seems to be a duty that my body takes seriously. Step after step, I traverse a desert seeming too vast to fully fathom, leaving a trail of footprints in the otherwise-virgin sea of sand, just as I have been doing for as long as I can remember. I think hard, but all I can remember is the sand, stretching off in all directions. I don't know why this is so and I don't want to think about it. I think of almost nothing, in fact – neither time nor place, discomfort nor pain – only that I am searching for what I had briefly attained and that the only thing I can trust is to put one foot in front of the other, for as long as it takes to arrive at whatever destination presents itself in this land of dun and heat.

In the distance, just a speck on the horizon so small that I couldn't hope to see it with mortal eyes, an old man waits. Unbeknownst to me, he has always been there, wrapped in a cloak too heavy for this environment, staring off into the unchanging sands, breathing the scorching vapors of this oppressive air, and waiting. The aged one raises a hand, beckoning, and I, so far away, somehow see it and alter my direction.

There is no time in this place, no way to gauge how long it takes for the old man and I to come face to face, but it doesn't matter. We are both here now, staring, waiting as if we have all of eternity for the other one to finally break the silence.

He makes a decision – I can tell by the language of his body – but still does not say a word. Instead, he raises his hand once again, lifts a single finger and makes a subtle gesture before turning away. It is enough; I understand I am to follow. With sudden realization, as though once again waking from a walking sleep, I find myself treading an ancient path that I was not aware of until this instant, as if it had appeared out of the sandy ground specifically for my taciturn companion and I. But I saw no such thing take place, so all I can do is accept this for what it is and trust what I know, putting one foot in front of the other.

Silently and tirelessly, my aged guide follows the sand-strewn, but well-defined, corridor through the desert and I, in my turn, follow him. I don't know where we are going and the old man does not choose to elaborate. I am focused on each step – heel, pad, toe, heel, pad, toe – the only thing I have any control over. As I watch my steps and the impressions they leave in the faintly-swirling sand, I notice that the feet of he who leads me do not leave any trace as my own do; I don't find this unusual, though it would be impossible to say why.

We travel for a distance before the venerable, cloaked figure stops at a spot seemingly identical to every other in the featureless expanse. He begins to speak, but he does not address me. I listen, but find that I cannot understand the words floating past me on the hot wind. I lose interest almost immediately, and cast my gaze down towards the loosely-packed grit at my feet, the feeling of which vaguely excites my attention. Hadn't I stood upon a path just a moment ago?

When the old man finishes, I look up again, expecting him to continue on our journey. Instead, I see that where there had been nothing but uniform sand, there is now a wide river, stretching farther than I can see, flowing sluggishly along, but sparkling in the vivid glare from the too-large sun. Something deep in my mind reaches out for the liquid, for the quenching of thirst I was not aware of until now, for the surcease of pain my body had rejected before, but that now tugs at the corners of my mind. The impulses are faint, however, and easy to ignore, so I do nothing but wait for a cue from the creature who has lead me this far.

The old man, for the first time, draws back the hood of his cloak and turns to me. His face is heavily lined and the skin is wrinkled and dry, like paper left too close to a flame, but he possesses a quiet vitality it would be hard not to notice. Despite his obvious antiquity, this man projects a sense of agelessness.

Again we stare in silence, each studying the other – it is not awkward, but rather comforting to be in the presence of another and not feel the need to communicate directly. Perhaps he is waiting for me to decide how to proceed. With this thought, a sort of understanding dawns, and the words creep from my mouth, as if afraid of being out in the open. "Am I supposed to go on alone?" I ask haltingly, pointing towards the river.

My companion takes his time responding and when he does, his voice is richly sonorous; a sound well worth the wait. "This is your place. I have no business beyond here."

Looking out over the listlessly flowing waters, I regard them a moment, then turn back out towards the sandy wastes we've already traversed. Like the path I am not sure if I remember, but still want to believe in, my footprints have disappeared, leaving no trace of the journey beyond vague memories. Turning back towards my guide, I say, "Thank you for showing me the way." Another pause as I am struck by a thought that seems somehow alien. "Do you have a name? So I can thank you properly."

The wrinkled man nods almost imperceptibly. "More than you can imagine, but you know some of them." And then he turns and leaves me behind, even more confused than I was before.

Alone again, I face the river, so wide I cannot see the opposite bank; part of me says there must be one and that my destination must be there somewhere. In reinforcement of this belief, a soft and faintly-moist wind rolls in from the waterway, brushing my damaged skin with soft promises I cannot quite decipher but want to see fulfilled. I inhale deeply, and within my chest I can feel the vibrations of a gentle, golden land spread out under a blanket of strange stars, conjured by a dingy imagination eager for change. It is the destination for which my heart has yearned, that my half-broken mind says cannot exist but my body tells me is almost within its grasp. Still, I hesitate, though my choices are simply to go forward or to go back. Even now, one foot in front of the other is all I am sure of and I choose once again to rely on what I know.

I place a foot into the water, unsure of what exactly to expect, and I am rewarded with a coolness that spreads from foot to leg to my entire body, soothing aches and pains I had forgotten I had until they are defined by their absence. My cracked, blistered skin falls away as I take another step, the water up to my calves now. Eagerly, I rush deeper into the slow, palliative fluid, further away from the relative safety of the bank that I am at least passingly familiar with, towards the unknown. Before I realize it, I am so deep that my feet, the only thing I trust in this curious and completely-foreign place, cannot touch the river bottom and I cannot see land in any direction.

I want to panic, deprived of my one source of comfort. Swaddled in this liquid embrace, however, my mind is clearer than it has been – clearer than I can remember it ever being – and yet still I cannot remember this land or how I have come to be here. I know, somehow, that I should be worried, but I'm not. I am instead possessed by a sheer and total calmness and bolstered by a strange urge contrary to every instinct I have. It surges forward from places within the core of my being that I didn't know existed and impels me to plunge into greater uncertainty. I dive, with no intention but to become somehow closer to this phenomenon that has made me feel whole and alive in ways I didn't know I was missing. With that release into the unfamiliar, I feel something enter me; something my waking mind could not conceive of existing outside of this place that must be a dream. Yes – this place must be a dream.

Now, secure in the knowledge that this place is no place at all, I surrender myself fully, completely, without any reservations or lingering fear, knowing that whatever happens here has no consequence. And in that moment, the breath of the universe washes over me, sending chills down my spine that radiate into parts of my being that are more than physical.

As I sink deeper down into the current, naked and insignificant, I realize that this is not a dream at all.

Lewis

Excerpted from the session logs and case report file of Dr. Jeremiah Fenster, M.D., Ph.D., Miskatonic University Hospital, Children's Psychology Department.

October 14th, 2009. Patient – "Lewis Doe"
12:34 p.m.

It's been about thirty minutes since I began my first session with the child the administration has dubbed "Lewis." As reported by other staff, he doesn't seem to be at all afraid, or even wary, of me but neither will he open up. Unfortunately, this is pretty much what I was told to expect. He's actually lost interest in me for the moment and is watching something out of the western window, giving me a chance to get this on paper. As if I'd forget any of it.

For the first few minutes, he seemed to be studying me as much as I was him – and far more openly than I'm comfortable with. At least it gave me a chance to observe him closely.

The physical abnormalities that Dr. Menton noted in Lewis's file (see section A-24) are readily apparent and he wasn't kidding when he said they were "creepy." Not a term I'd use, but I have to agree with the sentiment.

At any rate, before the hospital figures out what to do with him, they'd like an idea of where Lewis came from and how he ended up alone on that barge in the river, so I better give this another try.

"Lewis," my voice falters and I fidget, annoyed with myself because I should be projecting authority to the strange child. "I'd like us to try doing this puzzle together." I hold up the box and flash my brightest smile. I love puzzles; they're great for connecting with my patients. Unlike so many other things, they make sense – no matter how many pieces, no matter how difficult to fit together, it's something that can be solved. "Does that sound like fun?"

Lewis grins back at me, his too-wide mouth showing too many teeth – more teeth should possibly be able to fit in there. But he only focuses on me for a second before those weird, runny eyes start drifting again – in opposite directions no less.

I suppress a shudder. The disgust he inspires in me is physical. I've dealt with child sociopaths who seemed more human. I can't imagine having to do the initial examination when they brought him in. The thought makes me ill. I know he can't help the way he is, but still I want to run, to hide, anything to get away from this thing they tell me is a child.

Instead, I dump the puzzle pieces out of the box onto the table, keeping up a big, shiny smile I hope doesn't look as fake as it feels. I'm a professional. I can do this. I want to do this, even if only to prove to myself I can. Besides, after volunteering to take responsibility for at least this portion of Lewis's treatment – whatever that will ultimately entail – the administration wouldn't look kindly on me shirking those duties, so I've sort of put myself over a barrel.

Lewis's head turns back in my direction, drawn by the sound of the pieces scattering across the polished wooden surface. I try to encourage him and gesture towards the cardboard shapes. "Go ahead, give it a try."

There's no way I can possibly be prepared for Lewis's response as a whip-like tongue lashes from his mouth, snagging a piece and dragging it back to his maw.

The boy grins even wider than before, a ribbon of drool seeping out of the corner of his mouth.

I shift nervously and look towards the doorway. Sixteen minutes left in this session, then I'll go right back to my office and start my resignation letter.

Through
the
Ether

"It appears possible for man... to harness [the] ether and at his command... old worlds would vanish and new ones would spring into being."

— Nikola Tesla

April 21st, 1886 -

As vitally important as the product of a creative brain is to the development of both mankind and the world in which we live, more difficult than the birth of each idea is its successful transmission to others. I emphasize "successful" because as much as I can write, speak and demonstrate the foundation of my ideas on alternating current I cannot bring my investors to believe in my cause. It is all the more frustrating because without their backing, the Tesla Electric Light and Manufacturing concern we've built to date will go no further without their complete and total support. I know in my heart that this is the future — they just cannot yet see it.

I understand their objections — radical ideas are never initially well-received, no matter how well-supported — but isn't the mark of intelligence the ability to be persuaded by reasonable arguments rather than clinging to initial opinions that can be proven unfounded? These men, for all their business acumen, can see me as nothing more than the inventor of a clever new lamp. True, the venture has so far brought them profits, but I fear I will be unable to shake their impressions and gain the additional funds required without the promise of swift and impressive remuneration. And that I cannot do; no matter how badly I need their support, I will not stoop to lying to these men.

Still, I am not ready to concede defeat in this. The government has granted my patent requests for the new regulators. Surely if that hidebound organization can be convinced of their uniqueness and potential applications, my reluctant partners can be, as well.

May 27th, 1886 -

Has not man evolved past the need to rely on pure instinct? Have we as a species not gained the ability to allow our innate reason to assert itself and become on the whole ever more systematic and designing? As much as I believe this should be true, I am presented with evidence to the contrary.

I have met three times more with the investors with the same disappointing results each time. They simply do not possess the foresight or creativity to see the value in what I am presenting to them. Mister Arnold, in particular, seems to be dead-set against the idea of my AC motors. He brought up the failures of the many others who have tried in recent memory and presented his anecdotes as if such were evidence that the thing was not possible! I listened patiently, waiting for my chance to rebut his argument but when I had scarcely begun, he cut me off saying, "Mister Tesla, my gut tells me that it just cannot be done." More galling than his basic incivility were the nods and murmurs of agreement from most of the others. I give them mathematics, engineering and logic and they refute me with messages from their "guts."

Worst of all are the whispers I hear, circulating amongst the colleagues with whom I keep in contact. Edison, they say, undermines me at every step with a word here and a nudge there. I cannot believe that. For all his faults, Edison is a man of reason and learning. Such childish behavior is beneath him.

May 27th, 1886 (cont.) -

Happier news - I've received a trans-Atlantic letter from a gentleman called Ethan Layport, who is interested in my theories on wave-form transmission. I'm unsure where he has heard of my work in this particular field as I've yet to tell more than a handful of people, and published nothing, but he seems rather well-versed in the aspects that I've developed to date and quite enthusiastic. His commentary is among the most intelligent I've yet encountered and he seems to understand my work as well as I.

I will have to review some of my notes on the matter and give Mister Layport's epistle a second reading before composing a return missive. Already, even without knowing precisely what I will say, I find myself looking forward to his response. If nothing else, this was a most-welcome distraction from my current affairs and will perhaps lead to more interesting discourse.

June 4th, 1886 -

The past week has been a pleasant one after the previous months' trials and strain. I took a brief leave from the offices in order to refresh myself on the details of my thoughts on wave-forms and the ether all around us, which I believe to be their primary means of transmission. It is an odd thing to study one's own work, but eminently enjoyable.

As I read my notes and journals, I composed a letter to Mr. Layport and tried to put as much thought into my words as his own conveyed to me. I have read and reread his letter and find myself increasingly convinced that he is not only a kindred spirit, but perhaps a visionary in his own right.

I anticipate with genuine excitement his response.

June 6th, 1886 -

I have not been back to my "official" work for two full days yet and already my financial backers are badgering me once more.

I fear that my assertions regarding the U.S. government's patent-grants may have been a mistake. Lead once again by Arnold, the group now demands I build prototypes. I have proven to peers, colleagues and even the "eminent Edison" himself, during my tenure in his employ, that I need no models or prototypes. My devices are as real in my mind as they could ever be in the hand of a close-minded penny-pincher and, indeed, within my mind I can enjoy the purest forms of experimentation without fear or worry of waste or error.

I expressed to the gentlemen that the moment a device is constructed to carry into practice an unfinished idea that the details innate to the apparatus become so engrossing that the original purpose of the construction is lost. Results may be obtained but at the cost of lost quality, time and resources. Is not their primary concern financial? Is not waste of resources a waste of money? I don't think they can even see the hypocrisy in their request.

Prior to attaching myself to this particular group, I have never before encountered exception to my methods and I am vaguely insulted. Needless to say, I flat out refused the request.

I left the offices earlier than is my practice and returned home to try and relax from my confrontation. Mr. Layport's letter (the original, as no second could have arrived this soon) was inexplicably found on the table in the drawing room. I do not recall leaving it there, nor even removing it from the desk in my little office off the bedroom, but having seen it again I reread it and began to mull some additional points that had not occurred to me before. I become further convinced of Mr. Layport's erudition and feel that we would complement each other excellently as research partners. Perhaps, even given the distance between us, something might be arranged.

June 21st, 1886 -

Another meeting with the investors this afternoon. Beforehand, Mr. Weatherby took me aside and asked what compromise could be made between myself and Arnold, now acting as the de facto head of my ostensible benefactors. The man truly seemed like he wished to find an equitable solution and I hated to disappoint him when he suggested it could do no harm to build the prototype his fellows requested. I considered explaining again exactly what harm could be done but decided it would be useless. In the end, I told Weatherby I would consider it.

By the conclusion of the meeting with the entire group I knew that even that concession would not be enough for Arnold, but I finally agreed to his demand if for no other purpose than to delay the inevitable while I plan.

Much as I am loathe to admit, I am beginning to think that Tesla Electric Light & Manufacturing was a grave mistake.

July 3rd, 1886 -

Received a response from Mr. Layport today. He appreciated my answers to his questions and my comments on his assertions as well as adding many more of his own.

My theory on the cosmic rays emanating from the sun, as well as from more-distant stars, being harnessable for mankind's usage makes perfect sense to him and he did not dismiss or scoff at the idea that every exertion requires the permanent expenditure of life-energy – those rays being that of our sun. He goes on at great lengths about his own astronomical observations, some theories he has devised concerning the basic components and the types of energy that make up reality itself and how those theories dovetail with the physics of my own.

Layport closed his letter, in a language that came across to me as almost shy, with a wish that the two of us could work together in some fashion. I think I will explain my theory on the ethers in my next letter.

August 6th, 1886 -

The dynamo prototype, outfitted with my improved regulators, was completed some weeks ago and worked exactly as I had envisioned and designed it. I had assumed that this would be enough for Arnold and that I'd be left in peace for a time. Not so, unfortunately; now he demands greater improvements in efficiency and lowered cost, as well. When I asked if he intended to pursue my AC motor program, he said, "The group has yet to decide on that."

"The group"… and I had thought that I was in charge of this company's research direction. Arnold and his cohorts were intended to simply be a source of funding. I cannot see why they care so much as long as we are making money. After all, with or without the dynamo and the regulators and the motors, the company is still reaping profits from the light fixtures.

The stress of this situation is beginning to wear on me. My sleep is disturbed by unusual dreams so vivid they rouse me from my slumber, but upon awakening I can recall nothing but a sense of how life-like they seemed. I must take pains to distance myself emotionally from the day's events before retiring, if at all possible. Balance, as ever, is key.

As an aside, I've received nothing further from Layport, to my disappointment. Perhaps I put him off with the explanation of my ether theory.

August 17th, 1886 -

Several days ago, I awoke in the small hours of the morning drenched in perspiration, with my chest heaving and legs cramping as if I had run a great distance. Lodged within my mind was an inexplicable fright of a presence nearby that I could not perceive. With effort, I steadied myself and regained control of my breathing and nerves, knowing that it was almost certainly just the lingering traces of one of the unusually-realistic dreams I have been experiencing. Still, however, the sense of an unseen *other* within my private demesne could not be shed and I relented to my own foolishness and made a thorough investigation of my rooms. I found nothing, as I expected, and returned to bed still possessed by that irrational impression of not being alone.

A variation has since occurred nightly, though not nearly as terrible as the first such. I have forced myself to come to terms of a sort with my own troubled psyche, which allows me acceptance, if not relief.

Perhaps putting such troubles out of mind is best, though I know full well that this is dangerous mental territory. I must take care not to relapse.

September 9th, 1886 -

My days at the Light & Manufacturing firm are numbered, of that I am sure. Arnold demanded yet-greater efficiency from my dynamo and I explained that it was not possible to further improve my machine's production of electrical actions at this time; at least not with the technology available. He seemed to think I was making excuses and stormed out. I don't know how else to say something but the plain truth – the machine is already at its peak. Clearly, this was not the answer he sought.

It was only with the greatest restraint that I kept myself from expressing my thoughts aloud and further alienating Arnold, or anyone else for that matter. I have grown irritable of late, born from lack of quality sleep and the stress of my waking life.

I know this cannot continue much longer.

October 14th, 1886 -

They've done it. Arnold and his cronies have removed me from my position at the company that bears my name.

Arnold was prepared with some fiction about my standing in the way of the company's continuing technological development and financial progress. What could I say to that? The company would not exist were it not for technology that I invented and all present in that room knew it. Any statement of defense on my part would be ludicrous in the face of such attacks.

I don't know what I'll do next.

October 31st, 1886 -

Finally received word from Mr. Layport. He apologized profusely for his lengthy response time, explaining that he was so astonished by my last letter's contents that he wished to take the time to both properly digest them and to study the relevant material available to him so as to compose an intelligent response.

He proposed, in reference to my assertion that the ether around us has no easily-discernible qualities and hence has remained unobserved by science, that it is likely the same substance as composes outer space and that its very lack of properties is its defining quality. Like God Himself, Layport wrote, the only properties such a non-substance could have is what we attribute to it and that it would be up to us to find a way to imbue it with recordable characteristics. He suggested that since the ether would in theory curve light around large bodies, that perhaps specially-designed mirrors and some sort of light-generating device might be viable in capturing some measure of the thing.

I couldn't help smiling as I read the letter and I cannot adequately express how pleased and grateful I am to hear from a sympathetic soul. I will not, of course, burden my long-distance friend with my personal issues but something to focus on, even for a few hours, is very much welcome. This is precisely the kind of spiritual and mental boost I needed just now.

I believe it is time to propose a collaboration with my friend across the ocean.

November 14th, 1886 -

I could not delay it any longer. I have had to take a job simply to keep myself housed and fed. It is a sad, menial position digging ditches for a paltry sum that is barely sufficient to provide the absolute essentials – but it is only temporary, I pray.

My consolation is the sheer, scientific joy I feel when designing, in my free time, an ether-based experiment that Layport and I can work on together from opposite sides of the Atlantic. Though it has not been my practice to engage in such, I feel that this is a rare opportunity to work with someone who so intimately understands what I wish to achieve and I find myself unaccountably desirous of working with my mysterious friend. Almost compelled. No matter – the distraction is something I need to keep myself going. If I cannot provide myself with adequate physical nourishment, I can certainly still nourish my intellect.

I hope to have the broad strokes planned out soon.

November 23rd, 1886 -

I have no idea how on Earth it is possible, but Layport has already responded to the letter I posted on the 15th. I don't believe there is any way it could have arrived in England so soon, much less a response be carried back to these shores. I should think by sheer coincidence he simply sent a second letter shortly after his last but he addresses specific points from my reply. It is a mystery I will make note of in my return dispatch.

However, far more important than postal oddities are the contents of Layport's letter. Not only has he agreed unreservedly to my proposed partnership and to the experiment, as well as made some suggestions regarding slight alterations of my designs (which I believe will enhance our results), but he has enclosed funds sufficient to purchase the equipment and materials I shall require!

Apparently, my friend is a man of means as well as one of scientific curiosity. I thank my lucky stars that he chose to reach out to me.

There is still some time in the day – I had best begin gathering the required components!

December 17th, 1886 -

The apparatus is complete and with a portion of Layport's funds, I have telegraphed him to determine a specific date and time for the commencement of our great undertaking.

December 19th, 1886 -

It is decided – December 31st at 11:30pm eastern standard time we will begin. Layport's telegraph read, "We will usher in a new era along with a new year."

I certainly hope so.

I will arrange the equipment on the hill just east of the Tesla Electric Light and Manufacturing building out of a sense of irony. I think Layport will approve.

December 31st, 1886 -

It is almost time. All is in readiness. I can scarcely contain myself.

January 1st, 1887 -

I do not know whether to consider last night a triumph or a dismal failure.

The equipment worked, but the result was nothing like what I had anticipated. I believe the difference lies with Layport's modifications to my original designs, though I saw nothing that caused any alarm upon reviewing them when first proposed nor now when I have seen their results.

The device was configured properly – of that I am sure. The machine's purpose was to add a sort of artificial ultraviolet light into the composition of the atmosphere and, the light being carried by the ether all around us, allow said substance to be observed. I believed Layport's addition to the machine would provide a more efficient generation of the UV rays, which he had stated, but it brought about something else, as well.

At the exact time we had agreed upon, 11:30 p.m., I activated the machine and began to observe. The expected sputtering began as the machine warmed up then quickly smoothed itself into a low hum as I pointed the ray-emitter towards Layport's position across the sea, some thirty-five hundred miles away. After another moment, the array began to dispense a sort of pale, unearthly-colored light of a shade that I cannot describe for I had never seen it before and I do not believe it exists in nature. I watched, fascinated, as the strange luminosity waxed and waned, pulsing as if alive and carving a tunnel through the darkness towards the horizon.

As I watched, my surroundings took on a quality of hazy unreality and I became intensely aware of the sounds of my own body – the beating of my heart, the rushing of the blood within my veins and the faint whistle of my lungs each time I drew breath. Added to this was the undertone of the device's hum as it took on a deeper note, which seemed to reverberate outward from the base of the machine into the earth and from there into the soles of my feet, where it traveled up my body and sent tendrils of unaccountable fear into the animal portion of my brain. Added to this were shadows that seemed, no matter which way I turned, ever to be just at the edge of my vision.

Finally, heart pounding and lungs gasping with a terror I could not explain, I shut the machine off and sank down into the snow, trembling slightly and wondering what could have caused me such reactions.

I knew it must now be close to midnight, though I was sure no more than twenty minutes at most had passed; when I checked my watch, however, I discovered it was nearly four a.m.!

This period of "lost time" frightened me even more than my other unexplained experiences and I quickly packed up the machine and hurried back to my lodgings.

I have spent the last several hours pondering these circumstances and composing a letter to Layport describing my experiences, much the same as I have here. I have asked, as well, for any insight concerning this and his modifications to my designs.

Now, though I am loathe to close my eyes and chance reliving the night's events in dreams, knowing how sharp such recollections will be, I suppose I should try to get some sleep. I must report to my employer shortly after noon and I am sure he will expect me to be grateful for the half-day's holiday.

Oh, what a time of headaches and bitterness this winter has been, and it is not yet but half over. If not for the diversion offered by this collaboration, I'd have gone mad.

Though, after last night, I am uncertain that I haven't.

January 1st, 1887 (cont.) -

No time to jot this down before I hurried off to dig ditches earlier but, now that the evening is mine, reflection and recording seems its best use.

As expected, when I lay down to rest after my last entry, the dreams I feared arrived no sooner than I had fallen into sleep. Rather than simply a retelling of the events I experienced in the night, however, my brain ran wild with a story spun from bits of memories and fantastic images for which I can imagine no source. *Unlike* the dreams of the previous months, however, I retain a great deal of what I experienced.

I found myself back on the hill, as in life, and standing before the machine, which hummed happily as though it had been running for some minutes. The apparatus was emitting purple rays as it was designed to – though I should not have been able to view them with the naked eye – rather than the obscure light I saw in reality, and the air shimmered around the beam as it raced out of sight. At first I thought this scintillating effect to be the ether that I have always known to surround us, and that the experiment was a success, but I realized after a moment that what I saw through that hazy streak in the sky was not simply the mundane features of a New Jersey hill on a cold winter's night, but something else entirely that I could not discern quite well enough to fix in my memory.

I was struck then with an insane thought: what if, rather than simply cutting a swath through the night, the beam was indeed cutting into the very fabric of reality itself and leaving behind in its wake a tear in whatever makes up the barrier between this world and the next?

As this idea sprang to life, so did my surroundings spring into quite-unexpected motion. Before my dream-self's eyes, the immediate area began to melt and run, as butter left near a stove's flame, and pooled into a sticky, black mass at my feet that somehow did not flow down the hill as a terrestrial liquid would. From this arose, haltingly as if assembled by invisible hands unsure of their actions, a long, dark hallway lined with columns the color of the strange light I'd seen in the physical world and accompanied by the haziness the actual light had imbued to reality.

Before me, I saw that the hallway ran rail-straight along the path of my machine's rays and looking behind saw nothing but an apparently-infinite darkness, swirling vaguely and stretching away into unbroken nothingness. With no other option, I cautiously proceeded along the path presented me for some time without making any sort of forward progress, despite the movement of my limbs.

Chancing a glance behind me, I startled at the sight of an unknown companion who trailed me. He was black, though not a Negro, but rather a man composed entirely of an inky substance rivaling the depths of the stygian vortex behind the both of us, from which he must have come. Recovering from my momentary stun, and regaining my manners, I nodded in greeting and the fellow returned the gesture with an added, wide-mouthed grin showing blindingly-white teeth at utter contrast to the otherwise featureless expanse of his face.

Of the two of us he spoke first, asking if these were the results I had expected to obtain. Though his voice was cultured and pleasant, it chilled me to the bone for, without knowing how or why, it seemed to me to be the voice of my unseen friend, Ethan Layport – impossible though such a thing could be. Reminded by such lunacy that I was deeply ensconced in a dream-state, I shook my head and answered that more consideration was needed at this time. To this, the Black Man bowed slightly and said, "Of course, Mr. Tesla," and disappeared without another word, immediately after which I found myself awake.

Now, and since opening my eyes, I find appearing in my vision images of that unearthly man, that eerie hallway, and the light I should not have been able to see, as well as other things that caper maddeningly just out of my eyes' and mind's grasp.

Throughout the afternoon's work, thankfully mindless and leaving me to pursue my own thoughts, I reflected and analyzed. In my previous entry, I flippantly alluded to insanity but I know that not to be the case because what I am experiencing is strange, but not *wholly* new to me. The dreams, yes; the odd results of my experiment with Mr. Layport, yes; but the visions, of things I know to be real which seemingly cannot be, no.

As a child, I suffered from an affliction caused by the appearance of images, accompanied by powerful flashes of light, which marred my sight and interfered with my thoughts and actions. Most often, they were scenes of places I had never visited or seen in pictures, but knew to be entirely real. At times, I had trouble discerning what was actually before me and what was merely a likeness projected from my mind's eye. It caused me anxiety and mental discomfort and the fact that no doctor or alienist could offer an explanation simply worsened my state.

I could banish the images only by concentrating my thoughts and mental vision on something else entirely and straining to the utmost, but even then this great effort often only resulted in temporary relief. The scenes and sights would then creep back, blurred and indistinct but growing in concreteness, until I was once again under their affliction. I found that the only true surcease was to allow myself *into* these odd worlds, surrendering to their pull and making excursions beyond the small reality in which I lived and seeing ever more new locations in my phantom travels. On these "trips," I would sometimes meet people of uncommon dress and speech and we would share ideas and thoughts. Some of these I met repeatedly over the years and, strange as it seems, they became as dear to me as those in actual life. I told no one of these worlds I "visited," as I knew that it would be seen as a sign of serious mental defect, and simply hoped I would grow out of it, as many juvenile ailments seem to fade upon reaching the outskirts of adulthood. And, in fact, I was afflicted with my unique condition until I was about aged seventeen, when my body began to develop in earnest and my mind turned fully to invention.

I had never considered my childhood condition anything more than a quirk of my admittedly-unusual brain, but now I wonder... The events of the night, the grotesque dream world and my old "travels" have too much in common for me to consider mere coincidence.

Have I somehow been lead in the direction I now face? I have always taken great pride in my ability to identify cause and effect relationships but, like the shadows that pestered my vision last night, it seems just beyond my grasp.

January 2nd, 1887 -

The letter I composed yesterday to Layport has been misplaced. Not at all like me, though I am half of the opinion that it's for the best. What would he think of me if I were to send him such a mad epistle? I've instead used a bit more of the money he loaned me to send a short telegram asking after the results of his side of our experiment.

More worrying than my lapse in memory are the visions that seem determined to plague me. Unpleasant dreams, regardless of intensity, are troubling enough, but intrusions upon my waking thoughts can only compound my already-distasteful situation.

These intrusions, however, are nothing so severe as what I experienced in youth; rather they are akin to the motions at the edge of my sight when I was on the hill and again in the dream world I visit nightly. If I concentrate greatly, I can force these images to subside but when the opposite is true – when I consciously relax my body and perceptions – it seems that the air around me becomes filled with flickering wisps of living flame. This is not flame as is familiar, however, but rather dark and dancing tongues in shades of black from ink to a very deep Navy blue, not unlike the night sky when starless, but far less placid.

I find this much-disturbing as my old tricks of eliminating such experiences have only the barest effect and when I attempted to *enter* this vision, as my younger self was able to do, it resulted not in transport to a fantastic world but merely expansion and animation of the strange field. Within seconds of my focusing on it, sparks of scintillating green light, seeming somehow unwholesome, advanced towards me and left in their wake a system of parallel lines and closed spaces at right angles to one another; the combined effect of this seemed in some fashion to be an entryway to a far-off door I could not see. It was reminiscent of the hallway from my New Year's dream, but more abstract and yet, I sense, more truthful. When I ceased deliberate focus, the image slowly began to fade; rather than disappear, however, it transformed into a scene of the town, but all in shades of an inert and quite unpleasant gray. After a time it, too, faded but I simply don't know what to make of any of this.

Since that first attempt, I have been afraid to try again and have delayed normal evening habits by writing this, fearing what new and terrible shape my dreamscapes may now take. I foresee a night of cold compresses and fitful sleeplessness ahead of me.

January 8th, 1887 -

The one positive about my working days are the ample time in which I have to think. My employment offers no intellectual stimulation – though I suspect the exercise does me good – but nor does it prohibit my mental wanderings. Oh, and I have wandered a great deal these last few days.

Surprisingly, I have had no trouble sleeping, despite my predictions. I am, however, visited each night in my dreams by the murky man and each time he asks, "Is this what you sought, Mr. Tesla?" or "Is the data what you expected, sir?" Always he questions me with that incongruous smile beaming from his blank face and in a voice that my subconscious insists is the silent Ethan Layport, from whom I have still not heard either by letter or telegram. My response is ever consistent: that I have not yet determined what it is I am seeing, much less what it means. He indulges me with what I am coming to feel is an unctuous and condescending manner, though never becoming cross or otherwise aggressive in any way. After receiving my nightly answer, he disappears into the ether, as it were, leaving behind only the monotonous whine that in the world of solid reality came from the experimental machine's moving parts, but in this dream realm seems both sinister and almost organic, as if there were some sort of intelligence behind it.

Which steers me back to course and brings me, I think, full circle to the ether.

As I have described, I believe ether is entirely featureless and has no true substance. If it has no true substance, therefore, it would not be bound by any of the familiar rules or laws that govern this world. Might it in fact, if my conjecture has any merit, *not even be bound to this world?*

As Layport surmises the ether to be the pure stuff of which space is composed and in which all heavenly bodies are suspended, might the ether be not merely *around* everything but, indeed, *suffuse* everything – including worlds and realities other than our own?

New Year's Eve, on that frigid hill, I described what I saw as seeming unreal and indistinct. In my dream following that event, the sights and sounds I experienced were both more outré as well as somehow more concrete than what I saw with my waking eyes. What if that is, indeed, so? What if the device was not causing me to see things imagined but rather unseen things to be revealed?

Take for a moment as a given that my assumptions about the ether are correct, that it bridges some sort of gap between our world and perhaps many more, and that the device did as intended, imparting a measurable quality to the unknown substance and thus changing its properties into something new. By adding at least one characteristic to the ether, I may have changed all others and upset some sort of cosmic scheme, resulting in a sundering of what must surely be a carefully-balanced and ordered system and thus breaking down barriers mankind was never meant to even know existed.

Again taking my assumptions as at least temporarily true, this would actually explain a good deal and I fear what we may have done.

I must try to contact Layport via telegram again as soon as possible.

January 22nd, 1887 -

Still nothing from Layport. No letters, no return telegrams. I inquired at the Western Union office as to whether my telegrams had actually been delivered and the clerk assured me that they had been transmitted successfully and that his English counterpart would have alerted him had his office been unable to remit them to their recipient. I have no reason to doubt the man's word, but the alternatives are unsettling. Is Layport ignoring me? Does he think me insane? I wonder, also: does he share my experiences of these last weeks?

The phantasms have grown to at least equal those of my childhood, but I am powerless before their might. None of the coping tactics I developed all those years ago alleviates the experience in the slightest. I am now constantly followed by a swirl of dusky flame, and the onyx man follows me everywhere, at the edge of my vision, always just out of sight.

I sleep but I do not rest, for that same fellow hounds me in my slumber with his interrogations and no longer gives me the courtesy of accepting my rebuffs or protestations of ignorance as to the situation. He has yet to become opening hostile, but badgers me with his questions unceasingly until I wake, sweating and exhausted and more uneasy than when I lay down the previous night. The visions, both diurnal and nocturnal, fray my nerves and make even the most common of tasks challenging.

I must find a way to reach Layport. I am convinced that something was unleashed by our meddling and he has as much part in the release of whatever cosmic genie has been uncorked as do I. I know the machine I created could not do what that device did and I know his modifications are responsible – though whether Layport is consciously culpable or not, I could not say. Regardless, I would like to have his input so I may examine this dilemma from all angles.

January 29th, 1887 -

Made a desperate gamble and used the last of Layport's funds to send a telegram to the address of his rooming house, but directed to "landlord or lady," and inquiring after Layport. Received a response from a Mr. Edmund Rose indicating he had no such boarder nor had he ever.

I am a patient man, but even I have limits to my tolerance for mysteries and oddities.

Damn these visions. Damn Layport. Damn the ether, if it even exists.

Damn me, as well, for not leaving well enough alone.

February 11th, 1887 -

I am through with self-pitying. My situation is dire, but I have known adversity before and I did not bow then nor will I now. Though I am exhausted and it becomes increasingly difficult to focus my attention to a task, I will fight through.

Layport does not exist in this world, apparently, so I am at a loss as to with whom I have been communicating for nearly a year. Other than the missives I've received from him, I can find no evidence he exists or ever did. I cannot go to the authorities, who would simply lock me away, and my much-reduced position leaves me with few contacts or resources, none of which has been sufficient to the task of finding the ersatz English cipher.

That Layport's obsidian counterpart is real, however, I have no doubt. He has become my constant companion, whispering to me by day and chattering maddeningly throughout the night in my dreamscapes, his voice still smooth and cultured, but his words increasingly taunting. Last night he asked, "Why do you waste funds on the telegraph, Mr. Tesla, when I am ever within your reach?" then tittered evilly through those perfect teeth. I have long-ceased responding to him and his very occasional flashes of irritation at my impassiveness give me some small measure of satisfaction.

I sleep very little now but I have used the additional time to examine and reexamine ad nauseum the details of the ray-emitter that began this nightmarish affair and I have come to the conclusion that I will have to repeat the physical experiment. I have gone so far as to disassemble the device to its smallest, most basic components and still I cannot find any cause for the results it produced. There is simply nothing about it that is out of the ordinary or unexpected. I am quite obviously missing something, but I cannot for the life of me determine would it could be.

For the first time in my life, I am not able to create solely in my mind the results I need. My mental power has been so sorely diminished that I have even quit my position as a ditch-digger, though likely only narrowly before I would have been fired. If I can no longer scrape together the acuity necessary to move shovelfuls of earth, how can I visualize the inner workings of reality itself?

Now, I must rest as best as I am able. Merely putting word to paper exhausts me with the state I am in. Very soon I will have to take action and I will need every iota of strength I can muster.

February 14th, 1887 -

Whatever hand guides the workings of the universe has spun yet another unexpected thread into my life's tapestry.

I received this morning a visit from two Manhattan gentlemen – an attorney named Peck and one Alfred Brown, the director of Western Union of all things. They arrived quite unexpectedly at my rooms around ten a.m. and asked if they might treat me to breakfast. I did not feel up to an outing, particularly with strangers whose intentions I was unsure of, but I still retain enough of my wits to know not to turn down a free meal.

During our meeting they played coy, at first, but I am in no fit state of mind to dance around any issue or play at the politics of business and asked politely that they state their intentions. Attorney Peck was taken aback, but Mr. Brown seemed amused and explained they would like to discuss my going into business with them. As much as I would love to return to my work, and secure once again facilities and financial stability, I had to respond by explaining that I have an on-going "personal project" that I must see concluded before embarking on any new pursuits. I added, however, that I would be more than happy to listen to their proposal afterwards. Before Peck could say a word, Mr. Brown declared that sounded very reasonable and we concluded our meal amicably.

I hope I have not burned a bridge before even crossing it.

March 4th, 1887 -

The Black Man, or Ethan Layport or whatever he calls himself, knows what I intend. I suppose it is not surprising, since he has access to my mind other than a small corner that I believe I have successfully safeguarded using a variation on the techniques for my mental experiments. Suffice it to say that I have a plan and I dare not cement it in reality by writing it down should it not work. I do not wish for anyone to find this account and attempt to recreate what I will do tonight.

The creature does not know all, else he would surely brandish the information as yet another mental weapon and taunt me with his knowledge, but he knows enough to increase his attempts at driving me mad. He dances before my vision and whispers poison in my mind even as I write this. His presence has become so pervasive that I almost cannot remember a time when he was not my constant companion. If I am successful, it will be strange to have peace once again. I wonder if I shall even miss him, just a bit.

But I digress.

As intimate as we have become, yet a portion of my mind remains solely my own and I will not allow myself to touch upon those fragile barriers for fear of unintentionally alerting my enemy. He will know my full course of action only when I set it into motion. It will not be much longer.

I will not write again until I have resolved this matter. If, my unknown audience, this is the last entry in this journal then you will know that I have failed, though I suspect there will be other indicators, as well…

March 5th, 1887 -

It is the early evening, an hour or so still before sunset, as I write this. The past twenty-four hours have seen me engaged in a battle of mythic proportions that even I can scarcely believe, yet I know has happened from the scars my body bears. Or rather, it will when my wounds have healed.

But I know that this is real, and that I was victorious, because of the blessed silence in my home. I am free from the wordless whispering, the ethereal, unwholesome fire that has plagued my vision and most glorious of all, I am free from "his" sight and attention. My mind and my life are once again my own.

This is how it occurred:

On the night of the fourth, around seven p.m., long after the workers at the Tesla Electric Light firm had gone home for the day to begin their weekend, I returned to the hill east of the facility and set up my equipment once again. I had to repeat my "experiment"

– a word which I use loosely now that I know the results were never in any question – at the site of the original but I did not wish to endanger anyone innocent of involvement and so waited until I knew the area would be deserted. I was not alone, however; my tormenter had followed me, as was his habit, and grew excited to the point of hysteria, clapping his hands and gibbering in so delighted a fashion that were he a living, breathing man he'd have collapsed in paroxysm. From the gist of what little I could understand, he apparently believed that it was simple adherence to the scientific method that had lead me to repeat the process with which my troubles began. The unspoken undertone was that he thought he had succeeded in wheedling me into completing his own plan.

Once the instrumentation was in readiness, I settled down and waited until nearly midnight to begin, in the meantime trying my utmost to ignore my arcane harrier and center myself as best I could. This was due not only to recognition of the esoteric power in the so-called "Witching Hour," but the very-late hour would ensure no witnesses to the event. Once the device was activated, the sputtering rapidly smoothed into a hum which, shortly after, transformed somehow into a low pulsing that sent matching trembles both into the earth and down my spine. Interestingly, the moment the system was active the Black Man and his unearthly flames vanished from my vision. Encouraged by this, despite the tingling fear growing in the base of my skull, I allowed the machine to continue, ignoring the instinct to switch it off and cut short the infernal throb that was working its way into my very being.

Before my eyes, the device began to produce the same indescribable, save to say it was unnatural, light that I had seen months before. I stared, fascinated, as the edges of everything around me and, indeed, reality itself, began to take on a blurriness caused inexplicably by the recondite mechanics of my modified machine. And as the eerie light tore away into the night, ripping the sky with its passage, this time I did not look away. In spite of the growing numbness in my brain and soul, born of both fear and exhaustion, that threatened to consume me, I was determined to see this thing to its conclusion. Unexpectedly, I thought of my conversation with Misters Peck and Brown, to whom I had alluded to a "personal project," and chuckled slightly before regaining my concentration.

As I watched, the field of strange light expanded slowly but surely, throbbing like some grotesquely-huge vein, until it was large enough that it could have engulfed me had I been in its path. Scrutinizing the effect with as much detachment as I could muster, I noticed that when I peered *through* the weird luminescence, rather than at it, I was privy to a far different view than I should have been. Seen through the perverse light, the familiar world became an alien vista not unlike what I saw on my trip into the recent visions that haunted me, save that I knew now with certainty that I was seeing reality – no dream or hallucination had ever stopped cold the blood in my veins as did this.

It was a world of strange shapes, formed from precise angles, that was somehow counterpart to the world we know, for I vaguely recognized landmarks. Beneath a heavy blanket of stars in an unknown configuration, an analogue to the town lay. Rather than being peopled with ordinary citizens, however, its occupants were amorphous, blasphemous things that flopped and pranced and danced and capered to an unheard tune around the base of a gigantic, black throne the size of a large building and located where the town's square was in our own sane world. Upon this sat the most disturbing denizen of that mad landscape – a being of gargantuan size composed of a gray, pulsating and gelatinous mass which shook and quivered in time with whatever music the dancers cavorted to and which was covered in polypous appendages that nearly masked its most hideous feature: an eyeless and seemingly vestigial face with a drooping, drooling mouth. Despite its utterly alien nature, that hideous physiognomy held an unmistakable semblance to humanity's.

I was so enthralled with and disturbed by the images seen through this ghastly radiance that was somehow able to bridge cosmic gulfs that I had not noticed the light-field itself was expanding very rapidly now. I startled with the realization just as a strong wind kicked up and threatened my balance, carrying on it the faint strains of beating drums and whining, tinny-sounding pipes. Looking down to make sure of my footing as I retreated several steps, I then shifted my gaze back up to find that the Black Man, absent these past moments, leered sightlessly and obscenely at me from out of the abstruse and oddly-colored window my device was projecting into the sky. I gasped in surprise, which elicited a toothy grin from the creature – one which seemed to stretch the dimensions of that obsidian face outwards, widening to accommodate the showing of far more teeth than should rightfully have fit inside that jet skull.

Still smiling depravedly, the thing reached towards me from out of the sickly luminescence, beckoning with a finger, as a mother might silently call a naughty child. "Oh, Mr. Tesla," he said, his voice still unaccountably pleasant. "You had me worried for a time, but I knew you wouldn't disappoint me in the end."

Ignoring the unsettledness of my mind and the discomfort of my body as the thrumming continued to rattle my bones and the wind whipped my hair and clothes about, I set my jaw and replied, "So, creature, you think you have me figured out."

It nodded, its grin remaining hideously static while the rest of the head moved. "Oh, certainly, my good man. You are a *scientist!* And while your distaste for hands-on experimentation is well-known, you could never just walk away from an exercise in progress, could you? After all, an experiment performed only once is worthless."

It was my turn to nod. "You are correct, sir; at least in that regard."

A low chuckling spewed from between coal-colored lips. "And in what regard am I *incorrect*, Mr. Tesla?"

Demon or man or something else altogether, the being was enjoying itself and I hoped that, feeling secure in its victory, it was letting down its guard. I did my best to mimic its cavalier demeanor. "Before I answer that, may I ask some questions of my own?"

The soft laughter resumed, but faded nearly instantly. "Curious to the end, eh? Of course you may. I would expect no less of a man of your great intellect."

Bowing slightly at the compliment, despite its presumed insincerity, I continued. "You are too kind." I moved a step closer and gestured past the Black Man towards the exotic landscape behind him. "That world – is it related to the ones I visited as a child?"

"Very astute," its head bobbed as it spoke. "Related, but not the same, no. There are more planes of existence than even you could imagine, vast though your mind may be. Rest assured, though, that the worlds you visited are as a real as the ones you see now."

"And did you send those youthful visions to me?" Rarely does one have a chance to ask directly the questions of empyrean importance that have plagued his entire life; even in those circumstances, I would not pass it by. As I interrogated the thing, a hint of suspicion entered my voice, but if it noticed, no sign was made.

To the contrary, the creature seemed immensely amused by the question, and its grin grew somehow even wider as a fresh gush of laughter roared from its sooty throat. "You give me more credit than I am due, sir! Far more! No, those were all your own. Your brain is abnormal, to say the least, and you possess far greater abilities than any others of your species."

During our discourse the portal, as I came to think of it, was still growing, though its pace seemed to be holding steady, thankfully. I chanced one more query. "Thank you. I believe you are being honest with me, and I do appreciate that. If I may ask," I hesitated, as if unsure I wanted to form the question. "If I may ask… who are you, exactly?"

I expected mocking laughter or more sinister smiles. Instead, the figure leaned in close and practically whispered, the words all but lost in the gusts roaring around us. "Oh, no one but old Nyarlathotep." Here he gestured towards the monstrous being draped vulgarly across its gigantic seat. "Beholden to that great, drooling imbecile who goes by the name of Azathoth."

My eyes darted away from the face before me to sweep once again across the being even more dreadful than its servant.

"But you, Mr. Tesla," Nyarlathotep began again, "You can call me Ethan." And though it had no eyes nor any discernible features save that terrible grin, composed of those perfect teeth, I swear the being that I had once mistaken for a friend and kindred soul winked at me.

I don't know what another man might have done in my place, but in the face of that awful creature and the revelations I experienced, I suddenly felt saner than I had in many weeks. This being was not the cause of all my troubles, but it had preyed upon me in a time of weakness and exploited the core of my personality – my endless curiosity – for its own foul ends. I take full credit, however, and as with other mistakes, I intended to correct the error. I had to keep the thing talking to distract it from my purpose but, my curiosity sated at last, I also needed to move quickly while there was still something I could do. Even now, I did not know if my plan would work and so once again, I was forced to experiment.

A moment passed in which neither of us spoke; my gaze was locked on a point just over the creature's shoulder, somewhere in the world which it sought to unleash upon our own. Nyarlathotep, or Ethan Layport, or whatever it chose to be called, broke the silence with the oddly-human gesture of clearing its "throat," breaking my concentration as well, before speaking.

"Well, Mr. Tesla, this has been most entertaining, I assure you, but we've come to the end."

"Oh?" I replied, feigning coyness while subtly shifting my position slightly closer to the still-humming apparatus. I had never gone far from it, keeping it always within my reach, but now with the end indeed close one way or another, I would take no chances.

By then, the portal had grown very large – large enough for a man to walk through, though he'd have to stoop somewhat and step up over the small gap between ground and light. Nyarlathotep, close enough to reach through the aperture, now took a step forward, carefully swinging one limb fully through into this world. Seeing the opportunity I'd been waiting for, I acted and what followed happened very, very quickly.

I lunged for the machine in the same instant that the beast's ebony foot touched the snow-covered sward, sending up a gout of snow-steam and scorching the wet grass beneath. I flicked, in a very specific order, the series of switches I had added upon most-recently reassembling the device and as I did so, the throbbing, pulsing hum that had become the locality's vile heartbeat took on an immediate and drastic change. Gone was the sinister and unidentifiable quality, replaced by the steady, comforting sound of machinery at work. Simultaneously, the awful and peculiar light being generated by the machine morphed into a solid red beam that seemed to be chasing the ghastly streak out of the night sky and perhaps into open space beyond it.

For his part, Nyarlathotep instantly recognized my intentions and howled horribly, turning towards me with sudden pits of flame where eyes should have been, and I was nearly overcome with the almost-palpably overwhelming hatred they contained. The winds, already strong, whipped into a chaotic frenzy of destruction that swirled directly out of the being's mouth, tearing hunks of frozen sod from the Earth that battered my form and threatened to uproot me from my position.

I held on to my machine for dear life as that wild face came close, thrusting itself within inches of my own and shouting with the voice of the abyss, "What have you done?! Have I not shown you a world that no other man has seen? Have I not secured for you a place in history on a level unrivaled? And this – this is how you repay me?!" As the rant continued, the portal was shrinking with increasing rapidity and I feared that the Black Man would attack me directly and reconfigure the machine to its preferred setting, but instead he continued to alternately groan, moan, roar and shriek, to stamp, stomp, to claw the air before me and gesture angrily at the dwindling rift. Whether overcome by childish tantrum-rage or bound by some unwritten rules I am not privy to, the beast made no attempt to stop me directly and set its plans to right.

I admit that even untouched, I cowered before its fury – but I did not back away, continuing to shield the machine from the creature with my own body. Finally, it hissed, in a voice almost too quiet to be heard over the still-raging winds, "You think you are clever, little man. And you are – oh, you *are* clever – but not half so much as you believe. You think I am stymied, but I am merely *delayed*!" The thing moved so close that I could feel the heat generated by its black, roiling hide and it jabbed a claw into my face, only millimeters from actual contact. "You fancy time and space, form and matter are concrete but I know depths that mortal minds cannot fathom, and I know the ins and outs of reality. Someday, someone of your race will probe those secrets as you have and draw my attention once again. Whether tomorrow, next century or a millennium from now, I will win out for there will not always be a Nikola Tesla to stop me." Here, it chanced a look at the portal, so small now that only a thin strip of that other world was within sight, before turning back to me one final time. "Go on – warn your simpering little species. Tell them of the Crawling Chaos! They'll think you mad and the name 'Tesla' will be laughed at for generations. Either way, I *will win out*!"

Finished with its diatribe, Nyarlathotep's form dissolved into a dark, swirling mass that flowed into the pin-point fissure that remained just before it winked out of existence like some cabalistic eye of the world shut, at least temporarily, away. And as it went, I heard somewhere in the back of my mind a horrible whisper that said, "I should have chosen Edison!"

With that, the world returned to a familiar state just as the sun began to rise and I mercifully sank into unconsciousness and the first peaceful rest I have had in the year 1887.

When I awoke battered, cold and sore but also joyous and lighthearted, I surveyed the area. Other than the melted snow, chunks of torn sod and the odd burn marks, there was no evidence of my encounter and I smiled, uncontrollably and broadly. I disassembled my machine into its base components, destroyed each in its turn, then packed the detritus up and returned here to record my ordeal.

While I am glad that my time of torment is over, I cannot help but feel a strange sense of loss. Though I know it was nothing more than a cruel ruse, the letters from "Ethan Layport" came at a time when I truly, desperately needed some impetus to keep myself going.

I have fallen into despair before and I know that without the stimulation and excitement those missives brought into my life, I would surely have retreated into a state not unlike the one I experienced during my breakdown after university. The world seemed against me at every turn, and yet one kindred spirit rose up to shine a light of deliverance that I stepped eagerly into. Of course, that was the most malicious part of that unclean thing's designs, but still some good came of it and so I mourn what could have been, for had he been genuine, I believe "Ethan Layport" could have been exactly what he seemed – a friend and fellow with whom I could have gladly and productively explored the workings of our universe. Perhaps I shall encounter such a person one of these days.

Now, I believe, I shall spend what remains of this fine Saturday catching up on some sorely-needed rest.

March 17th, 1887 -

Attorney Peck and Mr. Brown have just left my rooms after a lively and exciting morning of discussion. They are extremely interested in the possibility of my developing the AC motors that I hold so dear and we three have agreed to go into business. I shall have my own lab again and they have pledged as much financial backing as I could possibly need!

I can scarcely contain my excitement. After all that has happened, I knew I was bound for some good turn. After all, modesty aside, does not saving the world deserve some reward? I jest, of course, but even if no other living soul ever comes into possession of this journal and the tale contained within, I feel that whatever governs the cosmos knows what has occurred and takes care to ensure balance.

And who knows? Perhaps more good will come of my tribulations. These experiences will surely generate some new and interesting areas of study. I've already conceived of a number of ideas and they continue to gush forth from the recesses of my own half-explored brain in the form of unshaped notions, glimpses of machines I've yet to design and words for which I have no definition. Some of these things are so strange and audacious that I wonder wherever they could have come from. An idea concerning rotating magnetic fields to power an engine is merely an extension of concepts I've been pondering for some time, but others seem like nothing I've ever heard or conceived of before and are so unconventional it's nearly as though they belong to someone else.

For example, whatever could the words *Cthulhu fhtagn* mean?

About the Author

Brandon Barrows lives in the shadow-haunted hills of Vermont, the last bastion of Lovecraft's New England, with his wife and a pair of elder spawn cats, writing comic books, prose and poetry.

His detective comic series JACK HAMMER is published by Action Lab Comics and VOYAGA, a science fiction graphic novel, was published by AAM/Markosia, both with art by Ionic. His horror one-shot RED RUN was published by Alterna Comics and he has contributed to the *New York Times*-bestselling anthology FUBAR from FUBAR Press. He has also had comics work published by or forthcoming from such other publishers as 215 Ink, Reasonably Priced Comics, Fan-Atic Press, Grim Crew, Monsterverse Entertainment and more.

His prose work has appeared in the book anthologies *Whispers from the Abyss* from 01 Publishing and *Another 100 Horrors* from Cruentus Libri Press as well as magazines/webzines such as *Sorcerous, Mystic Signals, Fiction365, Voluted Tales, One-Forty Fiction, The Were-Traveler, Linguistic Erosion, Daily Love* and others.

His poetry has appeared in magazines such as *FrostFire Worlds* and multiple issues of *Scifaikuest*, including being chosen as the featured poet of the February 2014 issue.

Find more at **www.brandonbarrowscomics.com** and for daily updates follow him at **https://www.twitter.com/brandonbarrows**.